A MIND'S EYE VIEW

Kzanol thought he was insane. Suddenly he was in the body of an alien called Greenberg, swamped by a flood of Greenberg's memories.

He suddenly noticed other aliens in the room with him, and they were coming toward him. But he couldn't tap them . . . he had no control over their minds. Had he lost *the* Power? Without that Power, a thrint was no longer a member of the race that enslaves galaxies . . . he was merely a worthless ptavv.

The aliens were getting closer . . . calling Greenberg's name.

Kzanol carefully manipulated Greenberg's unfamiliar body—and reached for the disintegrator!

Also by Larry Niven on the Ballantine Books list:

A HOLE IN SPACE

NEUTRON STAR

THE PROTECTOR

RINGWORLD

A GIFT FROM EARTH

TALES OF KNOWN SPACE:
The Universe of Larry Niven

FLIGHT OF THE HORSE

available at your local bookstore

WORLD OF PTAVVS

Larry Niven

BALLANTINE BOOKS • NEW YORK

SBN 345-24591-1-150

First U.S. Printing: August, 1966
Fourth U.S. Printing: September, 1975

First Canadian Printing: September, 1966
Second Canadian Printing: August, 1971

Cover painting by Rick Sternbach
Inside cover art by Bonnie Dalzell

Printed in the United States of America

BALLANTINE BOOKS
A Division of Random House, Inc.
201 East 50th Street, New York, N.Y. 10022

―――――――――――――

⚬₩⚬

There was a moment so short that it had never been successfully measured, yet always far too long. For that moment it seemed that every mind in the universe, every mind that had ever been or that would ever be, was screaming its deepest emotions at him.

Then it was over. The stars had changed again.

Even for Kzanol, who was a good astrogator, there was no point in trying to guess where the ship was now. At .93 lights, the speed at which the average mass of the universe becomes great enough to permit entry into hyperspace, the stars become unrecognizable. Ahead they flared painful blue-white. Behind they were dull red, like a scattered coal fire. To the sides they were compressed and flattened into tiny lenses. So Kzanol sucked a gnal until the ship's brain board made a thudding sound, then went to look.

The brain screen said, "Reestimate of trip time to Thrintun: 1.72 days."

Not good, he decided. He should have come out much closer to Thrintun. But luck, more than skill, decided when a hyperspace ship would make port. The Principle of Uncertainty is the law of hyperspace. There was no need to be impatient. It would be several hours before the fusor recharged the battery.

Kzanol swung his chair around so he could see the

star map on the rear wall. The sapphire pin seemed to twinkle and gleam across the length of the cabin. For a moment he basked in its radiance, the radiance of unlimited wealth. Then he jumped up and began typing on the brain board.

Sure there was reason to be impatient! Even now somebody with a map just like his, and a pin where Kzanol had inserted his sapphire marker, might be racing to put in a claim. The control of an entire slave world, for all of Kzanol's lifetime, was his rightful property; but only if he reached Thrintun first.

He typed: "How long to recharge the battery?"

The brain board thudded almost at once. But Kzanol was never to know the answer.

Suddenly a blinding light shone through the back window. Kzanol's chair flattened into a couch, a loud musical note rang, and there was pressure. Terrible pressure. The ship wasn't ever supposed to use that high an acceleration. It lasted for about five seconds. Then—

There was a sound like two lead doors being slapped together, with the ship between them.

The pressure eased. Kzanol got to his feet and peered out the rear window at the incandescent cloud that had been his fusor. A machine has no mind to read; you never know when it's going to betray you—

The brain board thudded.

He read, "Time to recharge battery:" followed by the spiral hieroglyph, the sign of infinity.

With his face pressed against the molded diamond pane, Kzanol watched the burning power plant fade among the stars. The brain must have dropped it the moment it became dangerous. That was why it had been trailed half a mile behind the ship: because fusors sometimes exploded. Just before he lost sight of it altogether, the light flared again into something brighter than a sun.

Thud, said the brain. Kzanol read, "Reestimate of trip time to Thrintun:" followed by a spiral.

6

The shock wave from the far explosion reached the ship. It sounded like a distant door slamming.

There was no hurry now. For a long time Kzanol stood before his wall map, gazing at the sapphire pin.

The tiny star in the tiny jewel winked back at him, speaking of two billion slaves and a fully industrialized world waiting to serve him; speaking of more wealth and power than even his grandfather, the great Racarliw, had known; speaking of hundreds of mates and tens of thousands of personal retainers to serve his every whim during his long, lazy life. He was chain-sucking, and the eating tendrils at the corners of his mouth writhed without his knowledge, like embattled earthworms. Useless regrets filled his mind.

His grandfather should have sold the plantation when Plorn's tnuctip slaves produced antigravity. Plorn could and should have been assassinated in time. Kzanol should have stayed on Thrintun, even if he had to slave it for a living. He should have bought a spare fusor instead of that extra suit and the deluxe crash couch and the scent score on the air plant and, with his last commercial, the sapphire pin.

There had been a day when he'd sat clutching a blue-green plastic cord which would make him a spacecraft owner or a jobless pauper. Bowed white skeletal shapes had raced round and round him: mutated racing viprin, the fastest animal anywhere in the galaxy. But, by the Power! Kzanol's was faster than all the rest. If only he'd thrown away that thread . . .

For a time he relived his life on the vast stage tree plantation where he had become an adult. Kzathit Stage Logs, with its virtual monopoly on solid fuel takeoff logs, now gone forever. If only he were there now . . .

But Kzathit Stage Logs had been a spaceport landing field for almost ten years.

He went to the locker and put on his suit. There were two suits there, including the spare he'd bought in case

7

one ceased to function. Stupid. If the suit failed he'd have been dead anyway.

He ran a massive, stubby finger around the panic button on his chest. He'd have to use it soon; but not yet. There were things to do first. He wanted the best possible chance of survival.

At the brain board he typed: "Compute a course for any civilized planet, minimum trip time. Give trip time."

The brain purred happily to itself. Sometimes Kzanol thought it was happy only when it was working hard. He often tried to guess at the emotionless thoughts of the machine. It bothered him that he couldn't read its mind. Sometimes he even worried about his inability to give it orders except through the brain board. Perhaps it was too alien, he thought; thrintun had never made contact with other than protoplasmic life. While he waited for his answer he experimentally tried to reach the rescue switch on his back.

He hadn't a chance; but that was the least of his worries. When he pushed the panic button the suit stasis field would go on, and time would cease to flow inside his suit. Only the rescue switch would protrude from the field. It had been placed so that Kzanol's rescuer, not Kzanol, could reach it.

Thud! The screen said, "No solution."

Nonsense! The battery had a tremendous potential. Even after a hyperspace jump it must still have enough energy to aim the ship at some civilized planet. Why would the brain . . . ?

Then he understood. The ship had power, probably, to reach several worlds, but not to slow him down to the speed of any known world. Well, that was all right. In his stasis field Kzanol wouldn't care how hard he hit. He typed: "Do not consider decrease of velocity upon arrival. Plot course for any civilized planet. Minimize trip time."

The answer took only a few seconds. "Trip time to Awtprun 72 Thrintun years 100.48 days."

Awtprun. Well, it didn't matter where he landed; he could hop a ship for Thrintun as soon as they turned off his field generator. Would some other prospector find Racarliwun in seventy-two years? Probably.

Spirit of the Power! Hurriedly he typed: "Cancel course to Awtprun." Then he sagged back in his chair, appalled at his narrow escape.

If he had hit Awtprun at more than nine-tenths light, he could have killed upward of a million people. That was assuming he hit an ocean! The shock wave would knock every flying thing out of the air for a thousand miles around and scour the land clean, sink islands, tear down buildings half around the world.

For a blunder like that, he'd draw death after a year of torture. Torture in the hands of a telepathic, highly scientific society was a horrible thing. Biology students would watch, scribbling furiously, while members of the Penalty Board carefully traced his nervous system with stimulators . . .

Gradually his predicament became clear to him. He couldn't land on a civilized planet. All right. But he couldn't land on a slave planet either; he'd be certain to knock down a few overseers' palaces, as well as killing billions of commercials' worth of slaves.

Perhaps he could aim to go through a system, hoping that the enlarged mass of his ship would be noticed? But he dared not do that. To stay in space was literally unthinkable. Why, he might go right out of the galaxy! He saw himself lost forever between the island universes, the ship disintegrating around him, the rescue button being worn down to a small shiny spot by interstellar dust . . . No!

Gently he rubbed his closed eyes with an eating tendril. Could he land on a moon? If he hit a moon hard enough, the flash might be seen. But the brain wasn't good enough to get him there, not at such a distance. A moon's orbit is a twisty thing, and he'd have to hit the moon of a civilized planet. Awtprun was the closest, and Awtprun was much too far.

And to top it off, he realized, he was sucking his last gnal. He sat there feeling sorry for himself until it was gone, then began to pace the floor.

Of course!

He stood stock still in the middle of the cabin, thinking out his inspiration, looking for the flaw. He couldn't find one. Hurriedly he tapped at the brain board: "Compute course for a food planet minimizing trip time. Ship need not slow on arrival. Give details."

His eating tendrils hung limp, relaxed. It's going to be all right, he thought, and meant it.

ᘓᗧᗣᗤᘖ

For protoplasmic life forms, there are not many habitable planets in the galaxy. Nature makes an unreasonable number of conditions. To insure the right composition of atmosphere, the planet must be exactly the right distance from a G type sun, must be exactly the right size, and must have a freakishly oversized moon in its sky. The purpose of the moon is to strip away most of the planet's atmosphere, generally around 99 percent of it. Without its moon a habitable world becomes shockingly uninhabitable; its air acquires crushing weight, and its temperature becomes that of a "hot" oven.

Of the 219 habitable worlds found by Thrintun, 64 had life. Seventeen had intelligent life; 18 if you were broad minded. The 155 barren worlds would not be ready for Thrintun occupancy until after a long seeding process. Meanwhile, they had their uses.

They could be seeded with a tnuctipun-developed food yeast. After a few centuries the yeast generally mutated, but until then the world was a food planet, with all its oceans full of the cheapest food in the galaxy. Of course, only a slave would eat it; but there were plenty of slaves.

All over the galaxy there were food planets to feed the slave planets. The caretaker's palace was always on the moon. Who would want to live on a world with barren land and scummy seas? Not to mention the danger of bacteria contaminating the yeast. So from the moons a careful watch was kept on the food planets.

After the yeast had mutated to the point where it was no longer edible, even to a slave, the world was seeded with yeast-eating whitefood herds. Whitefoods ate anything, and were a good source of meat. The watch was continued.

At his present speed Kzanol would hit such a planet hard enough to produce a blazing plume of incandescent gas. The exploded rock would rise flaming into space, vivid and startling and unmistakable even to a watcher on the moon. The orange glow of the crater would last for days.

Chances were that Kzanol would end underground, but not far underground. The incandescent air and rock which move ahead of a meteorite usually blow the meteorite itself back into the air, to rain down over a wide area. Kzanol, wrapped safely in his stasis field, would go right back out his own hole, and would not dig himself very deep on the second fall. The caretaker could find him instantly with any kind of rock-penetrating instrument. A stasis field is the only perfect reflector.

The brain interrupted his planning. "Nearest available food planet is F124. Estimated trip time 202 years 91.4 days."

Kzanol typed: "Show me F124 and system."

The screen showed specks of light. One by one, the major planets and their moon systems were enlarged. F124 was a steamy, quick-spinning ball: a typical food planet, even its moon's rotation was almost nil. The

11

moon seemed overlarge, but also overdistant. An outer planet made Kzanol gasp in admiration. It was ringed! Gorgeously ringed. Kzanol waited until all the major worlds had been shown. When the asteroids began to appear in order of size he typed: "Enough. Follow course to F124."

He'd left his helmet off. Other than that he was fully dressed for the long sleep. He felt the ship accelerating, a throb in the metal from the motors. The cabin's acceleration field canceled the gees. He picked up his helmet and set it on his neck ring, changed his mind and took it off. He went to the wall and tore off his star map, rolled it up and stuck it through the neck ring into the bosom of his suit. He had the helmet ready to tog down when he started to wonder.

His rescuer could claim a large sum for the altruistic act of rescuing him. But suppose the reward didn't satisfy him? If he were any kind of thrint he would take the map as soon as he saw it. After all, there was no law against it. Kzanol had better memorize the map.

But there was a better answer.

Yes! Kzanol hurried to the locker and pulled out the second suit. He stuffed the map into one arm. He was elated with his discovery. There was plenty of room left in the empty suit. Briskly he moved about the cabin collecting his treasures. The amplifier helmet, universal symbol of power and of royalty, which had once belonged to his grandfather. It was a light but bulky instrument which could amplify the thrint's native Power to control twenty to thirty non-thrints into the ability to control an entire planet. His brother's farewell present, a disintegrator with a hand-carved handle. He had a thought which made him put it aside. His statues of Ptul and Myxylomat. May they never meet! But both females would be dead before he saw them again, unless some friend put them in stasis against his return. His diamond-geared, hullfab-cased watch with the cryogenic gears, which always ran slow no matter how many times it was

12

fixed. He couldn't wear it to F124; it was for formal events only. He wrapped each valuable in one of his extra robes before inserting it into the suit.

There was room left over.

In a what-the-hell mood he called the little racarliw slave over from the storage locker and made it get in. Then he screwed the helmet down and pushed the panic button.

The suit looked like a crazy mirror. All the wrinkles remained, but the suit was suddenly more rigid than diamond or hullfab. He propped it in a corner, patted it fondly on the head, and left it.

"Cancel present course to F124," he typed. "Compute and follow fastest course to F124 using only half of remaining power, completing all necessary power maneuvers within the next day."

A day later, Kzanol was suffering mild gnal withdrawal symptoms. He was doing everything he could think of to keep himself busy so that he wouldn't have to think about how much he wanted a gnal.

He had, in fact, just finished an experiment. He had turned off the field in the second suit, placed the disintegrator in its glove, and turned on the field again. The stasis field had followed its metal surface. The digging instrument had gone into stasis along with the suit.

Then the drive went off. Feeling considerable relief, Kzanol went to the board and typed: "Compute fastest course to eighth planet of F124 system. Wait ½ day, then follow course." He put on his suit, picked up the disintegrator and some wire line, and went out the airlock. He used the line to stop his drift until he was motionless with respect to the ship.

Any last thoughts?

He'd done the best he could for himself. He was falling toward F124. The ship would reach the unwatched, uninhabitable eighth planet years before Kzanol hit the third. It should make a nice, big crater, easy to find. Not that he'd need it.

There was a risk, he thought, that the rescue switch might be set off by reentry heat. If that happened he would wake up underground, for it took time for the field to die. But he could dig his way out with the disintegrator.

Kzanol poised a thick, clumsy finger over the panic button. Last thoughts?

Regrettably, there were none.

Kzanol pushed the panic button.

Larry Greenberg climbed out of the contact field and stood up. His footsteps echoed in the big dolphin tank room. There were no disorientation effects this time, no trouble with his breathing and no urge to wiggle nonexistent flippers and tail. Which was natural enough, since the "message" had gone the other way.

The dolphin named Charley was lying on the bottom of the tank. He had sunk from under his own specially designed contact helmet. Larry walked around to where Charley could see him through the glass, but Charley's eyes weren't looking at anything. The dolphin was twitching all over. Larry watched with concern, aware that the two marine biologists had come up beside him and were looking just as worried. Then Charley stopped twitching and surfaced.

"That wasss willd," said Charley in his best Donald Duck accent.

"Are you all right?" one of the seadocs asked anxiously. "We kept the field at lowest power."

"Sssure, Billl, I'mm ffine. But that was wild. I feel like I sshould have arms and legs and a long nose overhanging my teeth insstead of a hole in my head." Whatever accent Charley had, there was nothing wrong with his vocabulary. "And I havvv thiss terrible urge to make love to Larry's wife."

"Me, too," said Doctor Bill Slater, but under his breath.

14

Larry laughed. "You lecherous fish! Don't you dare! I'll steal your cows!"

"We trade wives?" Charley buzzed like an MG taking off, then flipped wildly around the tank. Dolphin laughter. He ended the performance by jetting straight out of the water and landing on his belly. "Has my accent improved?"

Larry decided there was no point in trying to brush off the water. It had soaked through to his skin. "Come to think of it, yes, it has. It's much better."

Charley switched to dolphinese—or to pidgin dolphinese, which is dolphinese scaled down to the human range of hearing. The rest of his conversation came in a chorus of squeaks, grunts, ear-splitting whistles, and other extremely rude noises. "When's our next session, mind buddy?"

Larry was busy squeezing water out of his hair. "I don't know, exactly, Charley. Probably a few weeks. I've been asked to take on another assignment. You'll have time to talk to your colleagues, pass on whatever you've learned about us walkers from reading my mind."

"You sure you want me to do that? Seriously, Larrry, there's something I'd like to discuss with you."

"Squeak on."

Charley deliberately speeded up his delivery. Nobody but Larry Greenberg could have followed the rapid chorus of barnyard sounds. "What's chances of a dolphin getting aboard the Lazy Eight III?"

"Huh? To *Jinx*? Jinx's ocean is a foot deep in scum!"

"Oh, that's right. Well, some other world, then."

"Why would a dolphin be interested in space travel?"

"Why would a walker? No, that's not an honorable question. I think the truth is you've given me the space bug, Larrry."

A slow grin spread across Larry's urchin face. He found it curiously hard to answer. "It's a damn contagious disease, and hard to get rid of."

"Yes."

"I'll think about it, Charley. Eventually you'll have to contact the UN about it, but give me time first. We'd have to carry a lot of water, you know. Much heavier than air."

"So I've been told."

"Give me some time. I've got to go practically right now."

"But—"

"Sorry, Charley. Duty calls. Dr. Jansky made it sound like the opportunity of the decade. Now roll over."

"Tyrant," hissed Charley, which isn't easy. But he rolled over on his back. The three men spent a few minutes rubbing his belly. Then Larry had to leave. Momentarily he wondered if Charley would have any trouble assimilating his memories. But there was no danger; at the low contact power they'd been using, Charley could forget the whole experience if he had to. Including the conquest of space.

Which would be a shame.

<hr/>

That night he and Judy had dinner with Dr. and Mrs. Dorcas Jansky. Dr. Dorcas Jansky was a huge West Berliner with a blond beard and the kind of flamboyant, extrovert personality that had always made Larry slightly uncomfortable. Had he but known it, Larry had a very similar psyche; but it was housed in a much smaller body. It looked different that way. Mrs. Jansky was about Judy's size and almost as pretty. She was the quiet type, at least when English was being spoken.

The conversation ranged explosively during dinner. As Larry said later, "It's fun to meet someone who likes to argue about the same things you do." They compared

16

Los Angeles' outward growth to West Berlin's reaching skyscrapers.

"The urge to reach the stars," said Jansky.

"You're surrounded by East Germany," Larry maintained. "There's nowhere you can go but up."

They spent useless time deciding which of the eleven forms of communism most closely resembled Marxism, and finally decided to wait and see which government withered away the fastest. They talked smog—where did it come from, now that there were neither industrial concerns nor hydrocarbon-powered vehicles in the Major Los Angeles Basin? Mainly cooking, thought Judy. Cigarettes, said Jansky, and Larry suggested that electrostatic air conditioning might concentrate impurities in the outside air. They talked about dolphins. Jansky had the nerve to question dolphin intelligence, merely because they'd never built anything. Larry, touched to the quick, stood up and gave the most stirring impromptu lecture of his life. It wasn't until the coffee hour that business was mentioned.

"You were not the first man to read a dolphin's mind, Mr. Greenberg." Jansky now held a gigantic cigar as if it were a professor's blackboard pointer. "Am I right in thinking that the dolphin contacts were only training of a sort?"

Larry nodded vigorously. "Right. Judy and I were trying for a berth on the Lazy Eight III, bound for Jinx. I knew from the standard tests that I had some telepathic aptitude, and when we got the word about the bandersnatchi I knew we were in. Nobody's gotten anywhere trying to learn the bandersnatchi language, and there aren't any contact men on Jinx. So I volunteered for the dolphin work and Judy started studying linguistics, and then we put in for the trip as a husband-wife team. I thought our sizes would be the clincher. The dolphin work was just practice for contacting a bandersnatch." He sighed. "But this fool economic war with the Belt is fouling up the whole space effort. The bastards."

Judy reached across and took his hand. "We'll get there yet," she promised.

"Sure we will," said Larry.

"You may not need to," said the doctor, emphasizing his words with jerky gestures of his cigar. "If the mountain will not come to Mahomet—" He paused expectantly.

"You don't mean you've got a bandersnatch *here*?" Judy sounded startled, and well she might. Bandersnatchi weighed thirty tons apiece.

"Am I a magician? No bandersnatchi, but something else. Did I mention that I am a physicist?"

"No." Larry wondered what a physicist would want with a contact man.

"Yes, a physicist. My colleagues and I have been working for some twelve years on a time-retarding field. We knew it was possible, the mathematics are well known, but the engineering techniques were very difficult. It took us years."

"But you got it."

"Yes. We developed a field that will make six hours of outer, normal time equivalent to one second of time inside the field. The ratio of outer time to inner time moves in large, ahh, quantum jumps. The twenty-one-thousand-to-one ratio is all we have been able to get, and we do not know where the next quantum is."

Judy spoke unexpectedly.

"Then build two machines and put one inside the field of the other."

The physicist laughed uproariously. He seemed to shake the room. "Excuse me," he said when he had finished, "but it is very funny that you should make that suggestion so quickly. Of course, it was one of the first things we tried." Judy thought black thoughts, and Larry squeezed her hand warningly. Jansky didn't notice. "The fact is that one time-retarding field cannot exist inside another. I have worked out a mathematical proof of this."

"Too bad," said Larry.

18

"Perhaps not. Mr. Greenberg, have you ever heard of the Sea Statue?"

Larry tried to remember, but it was Judy who answered. "I have! *Lifetimes* did a pictorial on it. It's the one they found off the Brazilian continental shelf."

"That's right," Larry remembered aloud. "The dolphins found it and sold it to the United Nations for some undersea gadgetry. Some anthropologists thought they'd found Atlantis." He remembered pictures of a misshapen figure four feet tall, with strangely carved arms and legs and a humped back and a featureless globe of a head, surfaced like a highly polished mirror. "It looked like an early rendition of a goblin."

"Yes, it certainly does. I have it here."

"Here?"

"Here. The United Nations Comparative Culture Exhibit loaned it to us after we explained what it was for." He crushed his now tiny cigar butt to smithereens. "As you know, no sociologist has been able to link the statue to any known culture. But I, the doctor of physics, I have solved the mystery. I believe.

"Tomorrow I will show you why I believe the statue is an alien being in a time-retarder field. You can guess what I want you to do. I want to put you and the statue in the time-retarder field, to cancel out our, er, visitor's own field, and let you read its mind."

They walked down to the corner at ten the next morning, and Judy stayed while Larry pushed the call button and waited for the cab. About two minutes passed before a yellow-and-black-checked flyer dropped to the corner.

Larry was getting in when he felt Judy grasping his upper arm. "What's wrong?" he asked, turning half around.

"I'm frightened," she said. She looked it. "Are you sure it's all right? You don't know anything about him at all!"

"Who, Jansky? Look—"

"The statue."

"Oh." He considered. "Look, I'm just going to quickly make a couple of points. All right?" She nodded. "One. The contact gadget isn't dangerous. I've been using it for years. All I get is another person's memories, and a little insight into how he thinks. Even then they're damped a little so I have to think hard to remember something that didn't happen to me personally.

"Two. My experience with dolphins has given me experience with unhuman minds. Right?"

"Right. And you always want to play practical jokes after a session with Charley. Remember when you hypnotized Mrs. Grafton and made her—"

"Nuts. I've always liked practical jokes. Third point is that the time field doesn't matter at all. It's just to kill the field around the statue. You can forget it.

"Four. Jansky won't take any chances with my life. You know that, you can see it. Okay?"

"All that scuba diving last summer . . ."

"That was *your* idea."

"Uh? I guess it was." She smiled and didn't mean it. "Okay. I thought you'd be practicing next on bandersnatchi, but I guess this is the acid test. And I'm still worried. You know I'm prescient."

"Well—oh, well. I'll call you as soon as I can." He got into the cab and dialed the address of the UCLA physics school level.

❦

"Mark will be back with the coffee in a minute," said Dorcas Jansky. "Let me show you how the time-retarding field works." They were in a huge room whose roof contained two of those gigantic electrodes which produce ear-splitting claps of artificial lightning to impress groups of wide-eyed college students. But Jansky didn't seem concerned with the lightning maker. "We borrowed this part of the building because it has a good power source," he said, "and it was big enough for our purposes. Do you see that wire construction?"

"Sure." It was a cube of very fine wire mesh, with a flap in one side. The wire covered the top and floor as well as the sides. Busy workmen were testing and arranging great and complex-looking masses of machinery, which were not as yet connected to the wire cage.

"The field follows the surface of that wire. The wire is the boundary between slow, inside time and fast, outside time. We had some fun making it, let me tell you!" Jansky ran his fingers through his beard, meditating on the hard work to which he had been put. "We think the field around the alien must be several quantum numbers higher than ours. There is no telling how long he has been in there—except by the method we will use."

"Well, he might not know either."

"Yes, I suppose so. Larry, you will be in the field for six hours of outer time. That will be one second of your time. I understand that the thought transfer is instantaneous?"

"Not instantaneous, but it does take less than a second. Set things up and turn on the contact machine before you turn on the time field, and I'll get his thoughts as soon as he comes to life. Until he does that I won't get anything." Just like the dolphins, Larry told himself. It's just like contacting a *Tursiops truncatus*.

"Good. I wasn't sure. Ahh." Jansky went to tell Mark where to put the coffee. Larry welcomed the interruption, for suddenly he was getting the willies. It wasn't nearly as bad as it had been the night before his first session with a dolphin, but it was bad enough. He was remembering that his wife was sometimes uncomfortably psychic. He drank his coffee gratefully.

21

"So," Jansky gasped, having drained his cup at a few gulps. "Larry, when did you first suspect that you were telebaddic?"

"College," said Larry. "I was going to Washburn University—it's in Kansas—and one day a visiting bigwig gave the whole school a test for psi powers. We spent the whole day at it. Telepathy, esper, PK, prescience, even a weird test for teleportation which everybody flunked. Judy came up high on prescience, but erratic, and I topped everyone on telepathy. That's how we met. When we found out we both wanted to go starhopping . . ."

"Surely that wasn't why you two married?"

"Not entirely. And it sure as hell isn't why we haven't gotten divorced." Larry grinned a feral grin, then seemed to recollect himself. "Telepathy makes for good marriages, you know."

"I wouldn't know," Jansky smiled.

"I might have made a good psychologist," Larry said without regret. "But it's a little late to start now. I *hope* they send out the Lazy Eight III," he said between his teeth. "They can't desert the colonies anyway. They can't do that."

Jansky refilled both cups. The workmen wheeled something through the huge doorway, something covered by a sheet. Larry watched them as he sipped his coffee. He was feeling completely relaxed. Jansky drained his second cup as fast as he had finished the first. He must either love it, Larry decided, or hate it.

Unexpectedly Jansky asked, "Do you like dolphins?"

"Sure. Very much, in fact."

"Why?"

"They have so much fun," was Larry's inadequate-sounding reply.

"You're glad you entered your profession?"

"Oh, very. It would have surprised my father, though. He thought I was going to be a pawnbroker. You see, I was born with . . ." His voice trailed off. "Hey! Is that it?"

"Um?" Jansky looked where Larry was looking. "Yes, that is the Sea Statue. Shall we go and look at it?"

"Let's."

The three men carrying the statue took no notice of them. They carried it into the cubical structure of fine wire mesh and set it under one of the crystal-iron helmets of the contact machine. They had to brace its feet with chocks of wood. The other helmet, Larry's end of the contact link, was fixed at the head of an old psychoanalyst's couch. The workmen left the cage, single file, and Larry stood in the open flap and peered at the statue.

The surface was an unbroken, perfect mirror. A crazy mirror. It made the statue difficult to see, for all that reached the eye was a distorted view of other parts of the room.

The statue was less than four feet tall. It looked very much like a faceless hobgoblin. The triangular hump on its back was more stylized than realistic, and the featureless globular head was downright eerie. The legs were strange and bent, and the heels stuck out too far behind the ankle. It could have been an attempt to model a gnome, except for the strange legs and feet and the stranger surface and the short, thick arms with massive Mickey Mouse hands.

"I notice he's armed," was Larry's first, slightly uneasy comment. "And he seems to be crouching."

"Crouching? Take a closer look," Jansky invited genially. "And look at the feet."

A closer look was worse. The crouch was menacing, predatory, as if the supposed alien was about to charge an enemy or a food animal. The gun, a ringed double-barreled shotgun with no handle, was ready to deal death. But—

"I still don't see what you're driving at, but I can see

his feet aren't straight. They don't lie flat to the ground."

"Right!" Jansky waxed enthusiastic. His accent thickened noticeably. "That was the first thing I thought of, when I saw a picture of the statue in the Griffith Park Observatory. I thought, the thing wasn't made to stand up. Why? Then I saw. He is in free flight!"

"Yeah!" It was startling how obvious the thing became. The statue was in a weightless spaceman's crouch, halfway toward fetal position. Of course he was!

"That was when the archaeologists were still wondering how the artist had gotten that mirror finish. Some of them already thought the statue had been left by visitors from space. But I had already completed my time field, you see, and I thought, suppose he was in space and something went wrong. He might have put himself in slow time to wait for rescue. And rescue never came. So I went to Brasilia Ciudad and persuaded the UNCCE to let me test my t'eory. I aimed a liddle laser beam at one finger . . ."

"And what happened? The laser couldn't even mark the surface. Then they were convinced. I took it back here with me." He beamed happily.

The statue had seemed formidable, armed and crouched and ready to spring. Now it was merely pitiful. Larry asked, "Can't you bring him out of it?"

Jansky shook his head violently. "No. You see that unshiny bump on his back?"

Larry saw it, just below the apex of the triangular hump. It was just duller than the perfect mirror surface which surrounded it, and faintly reddened.

"It sticks out of the field, just a little. Just a few molecules. I think it was the switch to turn off the field. It may have burned off when our friend came through the air, or it may have rusted away while he was at the bottom of the ocean. So now there is no way to turn it off. Poor designing," he added contemptuously.

"Well, I think they are ready."

Larry's uneasiness returned. They *were* ready. Machinery hummed and glowed outside the cage. The dials were steady on the humped contact machine, from which two multicolored cables led to the helmets. Four workmen in lab smocks stood nearby, not working but not idling. Waiting.

Larry walked rapidly back to the table, poured and drained half a cup of coffee, and went back into the cage. "I'm ready too," he announced.

Jansky smiled. "Okay," he said, and stepped out of the cage. Two workmen immediately closed the flap with a zipper twenty feet long.

"Give me two minutes to relax," Larry called.

"Okay," said Jansky.

Larry stretched out on the couch, his head and shoulders inside the metal shell which was his contact helmet, and closed his eyes. Was Jansky wondering why he wanted extra time? Let him wonder. The contact worked better when he was resting.

Two minutes and one second from now, what wonders would he remember?

Judy Greenberg finished programming the apartment and left. Larry wouldn't be back until late tonight, if then; various people would be quizzing him. They would want to know how he took the "contact." There were things she could do in the meantime.

The traffic was amazing. In Los Angeles, as in any other big city, each taxi was assigned to a certain altitude. They took off straight up and landed straight down, and the coordinator took care of things when two taxis had the same destination. But here, taxi levels must have been no more than ten feet apart. In the three years they had been living here Judy had never gotten used to seeing a cab pass that close overhead. The traffic was faster in Kansas but at least it was set to keep its distance.

The taxi let her off at the edge of the top strip, the

25

transparent pedestrian walk thirty stories above the vehicular traffic, in a shopping district. She began to walk.

She noticed the city's widely advertised cleanup project at work on many of the black-sided buildings. The stone came away startlingly white where the decades, sometimes centuries, of dirt had washed off. Judy noticed with amusement that only corner buildings were being cleaned.

"I should have said, 'What do you mean, experience in reading alien minds? Dolphins have been legally human since before you were born!' That's what I should have said," said Judy to herself. She began to laugh quietly. That would have impressed him! Sure it would!

She was about to enter a women's leather goods store when it happened. In the back of her mind something slowed, then disappeared. Involuntarily Judy stopped walking. The traffic around her seemed to move with bewildering speed. Pedestrians shot by on twinkling feet or were hurled at suicidal velocities by the slidewalks.

She had known something was coming, but she had never imagined it would feel like this, as if something had been *jerked* out of her.

Judy went into the shop and began searching for gifts. She was determined not to let this throw her. In six hours he would be back.

"Zwei minuten," Doctor Jansky muttered, and threw the switch.

There was a complaining whine from the machinery, rising in pitch and amplitude, higher and louder until even Jansky blinked uncomfortably. Then it cut off, sharply and suddenly. The cage was an unbroken mirror.

The timing mechanism was inside the cage. It would cut the current in "one second."

"It is thirteen twenty," said Jansky. "I suggest we should be back here at nineteen hours." He left the room without looking back.

Kzanol dropped the wire and pushed the button in his chest. The field must have taken a moment to build up, for the universe was suddenly jagged with flying streaks of light.

Gravity snatched at him. If there were other changes in his personal universe Kzanol didn't notice. All he knew was the floor beneath him, and the block of something beneath each heel-spur, and the weight which yanked him down. There was no time to tense his legs or catch his balance. He bleated and threw both arms out to break his fall.

Jansky was the last to arrive. He came promptly at nineteen hours, pushing a keg of beer on a cart. Someone took it from him and wheeled it over to a table. His image wavered as it passed the cube; the wire wall couldn't have been quite flat.

A newcomer was in the building, a dumpy man about forty years old, with a blond Mohican haircut. When Jansky was rid of the keg he came forward to introduce himself. "I'm Dr. Dale Snyder, Mr. Greenberg's experimental psychologist. I'll want to talk to him when he gets out of there, make sure he's all right."

Jansky shook hands and offered Snyder a fair share of the beer. At Snyder's insistence he spent some time explaining what he hoped to accomplish.

At nineteen twenty the cage remained solid. "There may be a little delay," said Jansky. "The field takes a few minutes to die. Sometimes longer."

At nineteen thirty he said, "I hope the alien time field hasn't reinforced mine." He said it softly, in German.

At nineteen fifty the beer was almost gone. Dale Snyder was making threatening noises, and one of the technicians was soothing him. Jansky, not a diplomat, sat staring fixedly at the silvered cube. At long intervals he would remember the beer in his paper cup and pour it whole down his throat. His look was not reassuring.

At twenty hours the cube flickered and was trans-

27

parent. There was a cheer as Jansky and Snyder hurried forward. As he got closer Jansky saw that the statue had fallen on its face, and was no longer under the contact helmet.

Snyder frowned. Jansky had done a good job of describing the experiment. Now the psychologist suddenly wondered: Was that sphere really where the alien kept its brain? If it wasn't, the experiment would be a failure. Even dolphins were deceptive that way. The brains were not in the bulging "forehead," but behind the blowhole; the "forehead" was a weapon, a heavily padded ram.

Larry Greenberg was sitting up. Even from here he looked bad. His eyes were glassy, unfocused; he made no move to stand up. He looks mad, thought Dorcas Jansky, hoping that Snyder wouldn't think so too. But Snyder was obviously worried.

Larry climbed to his feet with a peculiar rolling motion. He seemed to stumble, recovered, tottered to the edge of the wire curtain. He looked like he was walking on raw eggs, trying not to break them. He stooped like a weight lifter, bending his knees and not his back, and picked up something from where it lay beside the fallen statue. As Jansky reached the wire, Larry turned to him with the thing in his hands.

Jansky screamed. He was blind! And the skin of his face was coming apart! He threw his arms over his face, feeling the same torment in his arms, and turned to run. Agony lashed his back. He ran until he hit the wall.

❧

A moment earlier she'd been sound asleep. Now she was wide awake, sitting straight up in bed, eyes searching the dark for—she didn't know what. She groped for

28

the light switch, but it wasn't in the right place; her swinging arm couldn't even find the bed control panel. Then she knew that she was on Larry's side of the bed. She found his panel on her right and turned on the lamp.

Where was he? She'd gone to sleep about seventeen, completely beat. He must be still at UCLA. Something had gone wrong, she could feel it!

Was it just a nightmare?

If it had been a nightmare she couldn't remember a single detail. But the mood clung, haunting her. She tried to go back to sleep and found she couldn't. The room seemed strange and awful. The shadows were full of unseen crawling monsters.

Kzanol bleated and threw both arms out to break his fall.

And went insane. The impressions poured riotously through his flinching senses and overwhelmed him. With the desperation of a drowning man trying to breathe water, he tried to sort them out before they killed him.

First and most monstrous were the memories of an unfamiliar breed of slave calling itself Larry Greenberg. They were more powerful than anything that had ever reached his Power sense. If Kzanol had not spent so many years controlling alien life forms, growing used to the feel of alien thoughts, his whole personality would have been drowned.

With a tremendous effort he managed to exclude most of the Greenberg mind from his consciousness. The vertigo didn't pass. Now his body felt weird, hot and malformed. He tried to open his eye, but the muscles wouldn't work. Then he must have hit the right combination and his eye opened. Twice! He moaned and shut it tight, then tried again. His eye opened twice, two distinct and separate motions, but he kept them open because he was looking down at his own body. His body was Larry Greenberg.

He'd had enough warning. The shock didn't kill him.

Gingerly Kzanol began to probe the Greenberg mind.

He had to be careful to get only a little information at a time, or he would be swamped. It was very different from ordinary use of the Power; it was a little like practicing with an amplifier helmet. He got enough to convince him that he really had been teleported, or telepathed, or some ptavv-sired thing, into an alien slave body.

He sat up slowly and carefully, using the Greenberg reflexes as much as he dared because he wasn't used to the strange muscles. The double vision tended to confuse him, but he could see that he was in a sort of metal mesh enclosure. Outside . . . Kzanol got the worst shock of all, and again he went insane.

Outside the enclosure were slaves, of the same strange breed as his present self. Two of them were actually coming toward him. He hadn't sensed them at all—and he still couldn't.

·Powerless!

A thrint is not born with the Power. Generally it takes around two thrintun years for the Power sense to develop, and another year before the young thrint can force a coherent order on a slave. In some cases the Power never comes. If a thrint reaches adulthood without the Power, he is called a ptavv. He is tattooed permanently pink and sold as a slave, unless he is secretly killed by his family. Very secretly. There is no better ground for blackmail than the knowledge that a wealthy family once produced a ptavv.

An adult thrint who loses the Power is less predictable. If he doesn't go thrint-catatonic he may commit suicide; or he may go on a killing spree, slaughtering either every slave or every thrint that crosses his path; or he may compulsively forget even the existence of a Power. The Powerloss is more crippling than going blind or deaf, more humiliating than castration. If a man could lose his intelligence, yet retain the memory of what he had lost, he might feel as Kzanol felt; for the Power is what separates Thrint from Animal.

Still daring to hope, Kzanol looked directly at the advancing aliens and ordered them to STOP! The sense wasn't working, but maybe . . . The slaves kept coming.

They were looking at him! Helplessly he cast about for some way to stop them from looking. They were witnessing his shame, these undersized furry whitefoods who now considered him an equal! And he saw the disintegrator, lying near the abandoned Kzanol body's outflung hand.

He got to his feet all right, but when he tried to hop he almost fell on his face. He managed to walk over, looking like a terrified novice trying to move in low gravity. The nearest slave had reached the cage. Kzanol bent his funny knees until he could pick up the disintegrator, using both hands because his new fingers looked so fragile and delicate and helpless. With a growl that somehow got stuck in his throat, he turned the digging instrument on the aliens. When they were all cowering on the floor or against the walls he whirled and ran, smashed into the wire, backed off and disintegrated a hole for himself and ran for the door. He had to let Greenberg through to open the door for him.

For a long time he thought only of running.

◦◦◦

There were green lights below, spaced sparsely over the land between the cities. You had to fly high to see two at a time. Between cities most cars did fly that high, especially if the driver was the cautious type. The lights were service stations. Usually a car didn't need servicing more than twice a year, but it was nice to be able to see help when you were in open country. The loneliness

31

could get fierce for a city man, and most men were city men.

It was also nice to know you could land near a green light without finding yourself on top of a tree or halfway over a cliff.

Kzanol steered very wide of the cities, and avoided the green lights too. He couldn't have faced a slave in his present state. When he left the physics level he had gone straight to the roof parking levels, to the haven of his Volkswagen, and taken it straight up. Then he had faced the problem of destination. He didn't really want to go anywhere. When he reached altitude he set the car for New York, knowing that he could change back to California before he got there. Henceforth he let the car drive itself, except when he had to steer around a city.

He did a lot of steering. The green country was more nearly islands in a sea of city than vice versa. Time and again he found narrow isthmuses of city, lines of buildings half a mile across following old superhighways. He crossed these at top speed and went on.

At one hour he had to bring the car down. The drive had been grueling. Only his mad urge to flee had kept him going; and he was beginning to know that he had nowhere to flee to. He felt aches and pains that were sheer torture to him, although Greenberg would have ignored them from habit. His fingers were cramped and sore; they seemed more delicate than ever. He was not mistaken in this. The Greenberg memory told him why the little finger of his left hand ached constantly: a baseball accident that had healed wrong. And Greenberg had taken this crippling disaster for granted! Kzanol was almost afraid to use his hands for anything. There were other pains. His cramped muscles ached from sitting in one position for five hours. His right leg was in agony from its constant pressure on the throttle during override maneuvers. He itched everywhere that clothing pressed against his body.

He brought the car down in the middle of a stunted wood in Arizona. Hurriedly he got out and stripped off his clothes. *Much* better! He tossed them into the right-hand seat—he might need them again sometime—got back in and turned on the heater. Now he itched where he touched the seat, but he could stand it.

He had been letting Greenberg's reflexes drive the car, and in the process had gotten used to the presence of Greenberg in his mind. He could draw on the memory set with little discomfort and without fear. But he had not become used to the alien body he now wore, and he had no slightest intention of adjusting to the loss of the Power. Kzanol wanted his body back.

He knew where it was: he'd seen it when he got the disintegrator. The Greenberg memories filled in the details for him. Obviously he had thrown the disintegrator when he put his arms out to protect himself. The body would keep until he found some way of getting back to it.

To do that he would need a way to operate the men who operated the contact machine. He would need a great deal of technological help to break the Kzanol body out of stasis; he'd seen, as Greenberg, the rusted spot on his back. But to get all this help he needed the Power. How? His human brain didn't have the Power in it.

But there was one chance. Humans had space travel, remembered Kzanol/Greenberg. Pitiful space travel: ships that took decades to cross between the inhabited worlds, and days even to cruise the planets of the "solar system." But space travel it was. If he could find the F124 system, and if it were close enough to reach, he could get the amplifier helmet. And Greenberg had had rudimentary telepathy.

The helmet could boost his tiny talent into a semblance of thrintun Power.

Where was he now? He must have missed F124, Kzanol decided, and gone on to a haphazard collision with this planet Earth. Where and when had he landed?

Could he reach the lost planet within Greenberg's lifetime?

Greenberg's body wanted dinner (it was 1:20 hours), water, and a cigarette. Kzanol had no trouble ignoring the hunger and thirst, for a thrint would kill himself if he ate enough to satisfy his hunger, and rupture his storage sac if he drank until he wasn't thirsty. The battle for food had been very fierce among the thrint's dumb ancestors. But he had cigarettes. He smoked and found that he liked it, although he had to fight an urge to chew the filter.

Where was he? He let Larry Greenberg's memory come to the surface. High school. History class, with lousy grades. The race for space; Moon bases; Mars bases. The Belt. Colonization of the Belt. The economics behind the Belt. Confinement Asteroid. Overpopulation on Earth. Fertility Laws; Fertility Board; Superman Insurrection. Sanction against the Belt, during an argument over the use of the Jovian moons. There was a lot of extraneous material coming through, but Kzanol was getting a good picture of the solar system. He was on the third planet, and it was binary. He had been extremely lucky to hit it.

The UN power sender on Mercury. Failure of the economic sanction. Limits of Belt autonomicity. Industrial warfare. Why was the Belt being treated as a villain? Forget it. Belt mining of Saturn's rings for water. Saturn's rings. Rings!

"Youch!" Kzanol hurled the cigarette butt away and stuffed his burnt fingers in his mouth.

F124. So this is F124, he thought. It doesn't *look* like F124. He started to shiver, so he turned up the heater.

At one thirty Judy got up and went out. The nightmare feeling had become too much to bear, alone in the dark. And Larry hadn't called.

A cab dropped to the corner in answer to her ring. She

34

didn't know the address of the UCLA Physics Level, but there was a phone in the cab. She had Information type the address on the cab destination board. The cab whirred and rose.

Judy leaned back in the soft seat. She was tired, even though she couldn't sleep.

The enormous pillar that was UCLA blazed with light; but these were night lights, to protect the structure from aircraft. Yet—a level halfway up was three times as bright as the rest. Judy guessed which level this was, even before the cab started down. As they swooped toward the landing balcony she noticed other details.

The big square vehicle was an ambulance, one with large capacity. Those little cars with the extended motor housings were police. There were tiny figures moving around.

Automatically Kzanol lit his last cigarette. His mouth and throat were raw; was that normal? He remembered that it wasn't, except when he had been smoking far too much.

. . . And then the Time of Ripening would come. Suddenly everyone would be in a hurry; Dad and Grandpa would return to the house very late and bone-tired, and the slaves never rested at all. All day and night there was the sound of trees being felled, and the low whirr of the stripping plant.

Before he was old enough to help, he used to sit beneath the guardian sunflowers and watch the trees go into the stripping plant. They would go in looking like any other mpul tree: perfectly straight, with the giant green flower at the top, and the dark blue stalk ending in a tapering tap root. In the stripping plant the flower and the soft bark and the tap root would be removed. The logs would come out shining in the sun, with nothing left but the solid fuel rocket core and the thin iron-crystal skin beneath the bark. Then the logs would be shipped to all the nearby civilized worlds, in ships which lifted on other stage tree logs.

But first there was the testing. A log was selected at random and fitted into the testing block. Grandfather and Dad would be standing by, each looking like he had sucked a sour gnal. They watched with single-minded concentration as the log was fired, ready to disapprove a whole crop at the slightest sign of misfire. Kzanol used to try to imitate their expressions. The little tnuctip technicians would be running around setting instruments and looking harried and important. They seemed too small to be intelligent animals, but they were. Their quaint biological science had mutated the stage trees out of worthless mpul trees. They had created the sunflowers which guarded the house: a hedge of twelve-foot trunks, each bearing a flexible silver mirror to focus sunlight on the green photosynthetic node, or to shift that focus onto an attacking enemy. Tnuctipun had built the gigantic, mindless yeast-eating whitefoods which fed the family and the carnivorous tnuctipun themselves. They had been given more freedom than any other slave race, because they had proven the worth of their freethinking brains.

A tnuctip would set off the log. The flame would shoot out over the valley, blue-white and very straight, darkening at the end to red smoke, while instruments measured the log's precise thrust and Grandfather smiled in satisfaction. The flame shook the world with its sound, so that little Kzanol used to fear that the thrust was increasing the planet's spin. . . .

Kzanol/Greenberg reached to knock the ash off his last cigarette and saw his second-to-last burning in the ash tray, two-thirds smoked. He hadn't done that since high school! He cursed a thrintun curse and almost strangled on it; his throat positively wasn't built for overtalk.

He wasn't gaining anything with his reminiscing, either.

Wherever in the universe he was, he still had to reach

36

a spaceport. He needed the amplifier. Later he could figure out why there were aliens on F124, and why they thought they had been here longer than was possible. He started the motor and punched for Topeka, Kansas.

He'd have to steal a ship anyway. It might as well be an armed ship (since this region of space was lawless by definition, having no thrintun), and there was a military spaceport near Topeka.

Wait a moment, he thought. This couldn't be F124. There were too many planets! F124 had only eight, and here there were nine.

Now that he was started he noticed other discrepancies. The asteroid belt of F124 had been far thicker, and her moon had had a slight rotation, he remembered. He was in the wrong system!

Merely a coincidence! Kzanol grinned. And what· a coincidence! The habitable planet, the ringed planet, the ordered sizes of the worlds . . . come to think of it, he was the only thrint ever to have found two slave planets. He would be the richest being in the galaxy! He didn't care, now, if he never found the map. But, of course, he still needed the amplifier.

❧

Judy felt that she was on the verge of a tantrum. "But can't they talk at all?" she begged, knowing she was being unreasonable.

Los Angeles Police Chief Lloyd Masney's patience was wearing thin. "Mrs. Greenberg," he said heavily. "You know that Doctor Jansky is having his eyes and face replaced at this moment. Also a wide patch of skin on his back, which was taken off almost down to the spinal cord. The others are almost as badly off. Dr. Snyder has no eye damage, but the part of his face that he didn't cover with his hands is being replaced, and the palms of his hands, and some skin from his back. Knudsen *did* have his spinal cord opened, and some ribs too. The autodoc won't let us wake any of them up, even under police priority, except for Mr. Trimonti. He is being questioned while the 'doc replaces skull and scalp from the back of his head. He has had a bad shock, and he is under local anesthetic, and you may not disturb him! You may hear the transcription of our interview when we have it. Meanwhile, may I offer you some coffee?"

"Yes, thank you," said Judy. She thought he was giving her a chance to get a grip on herself, and was grateful. When he came back with the coffee she sipped it for a few moments, covertly studying the police chief.

He was a burly man who walked like he had bad feet. No wonder if he did; his hands and feet were both tiny in proportion to the rest of his body. He had straight white hair and a dark complexion. His bushy mustache was also white. He seemed almost as impatient as she. She had not yet seen him sit in normal fashion; now his legs were draped over one arm of his swivel chair while his shoulders rested against the other.

"Have you any idea where he is now?" She couldn't restrain herself.

"Sure," Masney said unexpectedly. "He just crossed the Kansas-Colorado border at a height of nine thousand feet. I guess he doesn't know how to short out his license sender. But then, maybe he just didn't bother."

"Maybe he just doesn't like cities," said the old man in the corner. Judy had thought he was asleep. He had been introduced as Lucas Garner, an Arm of the UN. Judy waited for him to go on, but he seemed to think he had explained himself. Masney explained for him.

"You see, we don't advertise the fact that all our override beamers are in the cities. I figure that if he knows enough to go around the cities, which he's been doing, he must know enough to short out his license so that we

38

can't follow him. Luke, have you got some reason to think he doesn't like cities?"

Luke nodded. Judy thought he looked like the oldest man in the world. His face was as wrinkled as Satan's. He rode a ground-effect travel chair as powerful as a personal tank. "I've been expecting something like this for years," he said. "Lloyd, do you remember when the Fertility Laws went into force, and I told you that a lot of homicidal nuts would start killing bachelors who had gotten permits to have children? And it happened. This is like that. I thought it might happen on Jinx, but it happened here instead.

"Larry Greenberg thinks he's an alien."

Judy was stunned. "But he's done this before," she protested.

"No." Garner drew a lit cigarette from the arm of his chair. "He hasn't. He's worked with men and dolphins. Now he's run into something he can't take. I've got a hunch what it is, and I'd give my wheel chair"—Judy looked, but it didn't have wheels—"to know if I'm right.

"Mrs. Greenberg. Has your husband ever been asked to read the mind of a telepath?"

Mutely Judy shook her head.

"So," said Garner. Again he looked like he'd gone to sleep, this time with a cigarette burning between his fingers. His hands were huge, with muscles showing beneath the loose, mottled skin, and his shoulders belonged on a blacksmith. The contrast between Garner's massive torso and his helpless, almost fleshless legs made him look a little like a bald ape. He came to life, sucked in a massive dose of smoke, and went on talking.

"Lloyd's men got here about fifteen minutes after Larry Greenberg left. Trimonti called the cops, of course; nobody else could move. Lloyd himself was here in another ten. When he saw the wounds on the men Greenberg shot, he called me in Brussels.

"I'm an Arm, a member of the UN Technological Police. There was a chance the weapon that made those wounds would have to be suppressed. Certainly it needed investigation. So my first interest was the weapon.

"I don't suppose either of you ever heard of Buck Rogers? No? Too bad. Then I'll just say that nothing in our present technology could have led to a weapon like this.

"It does *not* destroy matter, which is reassuring. Rewriting one law of physics is worse than trying to eat one peanut. The weapon *scatters* matter. Lloyd's men found traces of blood and flesh and bone forming a greasy layer all over the room. Not merely microscopic traces, but clumps too small to see at all.

"Trimonti's testimony was a godsend. Obviously the Sea Statue dropped the weapon, and Greenberg used it. Why?"

Masney rumbled, "Get to the point, Luke."

"Okay, here it comes. The contact helmet is a very complicated psionics device. One question the psychologists have wondered about is this. Why don't the contact men get more confused when extraneous memories pour in? Usually there's a few minutes of confusion, and then everything straightens out. They say it's because the incoming memories are weak and fuzzy, but that's only half an answer. It may even be a result, not a cause.

"Picture it. Two men sit down under crystal-iron helmets, and when one of them gets up he has two complete sets of memories. Which one is him?

"Well, one set remembers a different body from the one he finds himself in. More important, one set remembers being a telepath and the other doesn't! One set remembers sitting down under a contact helmet with the foreknowledge that when he gets up he will have two sets of memories. Naturally the contact man will behave as if that set were his own. Even with eight or ten different memory sets, the contact man will automatically use his own.

"Well, let's say the Sea Statue is a telepath. Not a telepathy-prone, like Larry Greenberg, but a full telepath, able to read any mind whenever he chooses. Suddenly all bets are off. Greenberg wakes with two sets of memories, and one set remembers reading hundreds of other minds, or thousands! Got it?"

"Yes. Oh, yes," said Judy. "I warned him something was going to happen. But what can we do?"

"If he doesn't pass over a city soon we'll have to send up interceptors. We'd better wait 'til Snyder gets out of the 'doc."

⌒⌒⌒

Kzanol dropped the car again half an hour later. He had been wondering about the peculiar gritty feeling in his eyes, and when he felt he was about to lose consciousness he became frightened. Then his Greenberg memories told him what was wrong. He was sleepy.

He didn't even waste time worrying about it. Kzanol was getting used to the humiliations that came with Greenberg's body. He put the car down in a plowed field and slept.

He woke at first light and took the car up at once. And then, incredibly, he began to enjoy himself. Towns and cities appeared before the speeding car, and he circled them cautiously; but the countryside began to attract his attention. The fields of grain and alfalfa were strange in their small size and checkerboard design. There was other vegetation, and he dropped low to examine the trees. Trees with shapeless woolly green heads instead of flowers. Trees that sometimes hugged the ground as if fearing the sky. Perhaps the winds were dangerous on this world. Trees that almost never grew completely straight. They were weird and asymmetrical and beautiful, and the Greenberg memory could tell him little

41

about them; Greenberg was a city man. He curved out of his way to see them. He dipped low over quaint houses with peaked roofs, delighted by their novel architecture, and he wondered again about Earth's weather. Greenberg, jogged this time, remembered a Kansas tornado. Kzanol was impressed.

Kzanol was as happy as a tourist. True, he was even more uncomfortable, for he was hungry and thirsty and in need of nicotine or gnals. But he could ignore these minor discomforts; he was a thrint, he knew that a gnal would be deadly poison, and it had been Greenberg's fixed belief that he could stop smoking whenever he pleased. Kzanol believed him and ignored the craving. Normally he would trust anything he found in the Greenberg memory.

So he gawked at the scenery like any tourist doing something new and different.

After two hours it began to pall. The problem of where in space he was was worrying him again. But he saw the solution already. The Topeka Public Library was the place to go. If a nearby solar system had been found which was nearly identical with this one, he would find it listed there. The Belt telescopes, unhampered by atmospheric distortion, were able to see planets circling other suns; and the interstellar ramscoop robots had been searching out man-habitable systems for nearly a century. If the F124 system had not yet been found, it was beyond the reach of terran ships, and he might as well decently commit suicide.

Amazing, how nearly alike were the F124 system and the solar system. There were the two habitable binary thirds, the giant fifths, the asteroid belts, similar in position if not in density, the correspondence of size and position of the first eight planets of each system, the ringed sixth—it was almost too much to believe.

Oh, Powerloss. Kzanol/Greenberg sighed and cracked his knuckles, badly frightening himself. It *was* too much to believe. He didn't believe it.

42

Suddenly he was very tired. Thrintun was very far away in an unknown direction. The amplifier helmet, and everything else he owned, were probably equally unreachable in a completely different direction. His Power was gone, and even his body had been stolen by some terrifying slave sorcery. But worst of all, he had no idea what to do next!

A city rose in the distance. His car was making straight for it. He was about to steer around it when he realized it must be Topeka. So he put his head in his arms and wished he could lose consciousness again. The strength seemed to have leaked out of him.

This had to be F124.

But it couldn't be. The system had an extra world and not enough asteroids.

But, he remembered, Pluto was supposed to be a stowaway in the solar system. There was its queer orbit, and some mathematical discrepancy in its size. Perhaps it was captured by Sol before he awakened.

But in three hundred years? Highly unlikely.

Kzanol raised his face, and his face showed terror. He knew perfectly well that three hundred years was his lower limit; the brain board had given him a three-hundred-year journey using half the ship's power. He might have been buried much longer than that.

Suppose he accepted Pluto. What about the slave race, happily living where there should have been only yeast, covering the oceans a foot deep, or at most white-foods, big as brontosaurs and twice as pretty, wandering along the shorelines feeding on mutated scum?

He couldn't explain it, so he dropped it.

But the asteroid belt was certainly thinner than it had been. True, it would have thinned out anyway in time, what with photon pressure and solar wind pushing dust and the smaller particles outward into deep space, and collisions with the bigger planets removing a few rocks, and even some of the most eccentric asteroids being slowed and killed by friction with the solar

43

atmosphere—which must extend well past Earth. But that was not a matter for a few hundred years. Or even thousands. Or hundreds of—

And he knew.

Not hundreds of years, or hundreds of thousands. He had been at the bottom of the sea while the solar system captured a new planet, and lost a good third of its asteroid belt, while oceans of food yeast mutated and went bad, and mutated again, and again . . . At the bottom of the sea he had waited while yeast became grass and fish and now walked on two legs like a thrint.

A billion years wouldn't be long enough. Two billion might do it.

He was hugging his knees with both arms, almost as if he were trying to bury his head between them. A thrint couldn't have done that. It was not the pure passage of time that frightened him so. It was the loss of everything he knew and loved, even his own race. Not only Thrintun the world, but also Thrint the species, must be lost in the past. If there had been thrintun in the galaxy they would have colonized Earth long ages ago.

He was the last thrint.

Slowly he raised his head, to stare, expressionless, at the wide city beneath him.

He could damn well behave like a thrint.

The car had stopped. He must be over the center of Topeka. But which way was the spaceport? And how would he get in? Greenberg, worse luck, had had no experience in stealing spacecraft. Well, first find out where it was, and then . . .

The ship was vibrating. He could feel it with those ridiculously delicate fingertips. There was sound too, too high to hear, but he could feel it jangling in his nerves. What was going on?

He went to sleep. The car hung for a moment longer, then started down.

"They always stack me in the rear of the plane," Garner grumbled.

Lloyd Masney was unsympathetic. "You're lucky they don't make you ride in the baggage compartment—seeing as you refuse to leave that hot rod there alone."

"Well, why not? I'm a cripple!"

"Uh huh. Aren't the Ch'ien treatments working?"

"Well, yes, in a manner of speaking. My spinal cord is carrying some messages again. But walking ten paces around a room twice a day just about kills me. It'll be another year before I can walk downtown and back. Meanwhile my chair rides with me, not in the luggage compartment. I'm used to it."

"You'll never miss that year," Masney told him. "How old are you now, Luke?"

"Hundred and seventy next April. But the years aren't getting any shorter, Lloyd, contrary to public opinion. Why do they have to stack me in the rear? I get nervous when I see the wings turn red hot." He shifted uncomfortably.

Judy Greenberg came back from the rest room and sat down next to Lloyd. Luke was across the aisle, in the space made by removing two chairs before takeoff. Judy seemed to have recovered nicely; she looked and moved as if she had just left a beauty parlor. From a distance her face was calm. Garner could see the slight tension in the muscles around the eyes, in the cheeks, through the neck. But Garner was very old. He had his own, non-psychic way of reading minds. He said, as if to empty air, "We'll be landing in half an hour. Greenberg will be sleeping peacefully until we get there."

"Good," said Judy. She leaned forward and turned on the tridee screen in the seat ahead.

Kzanol felt a brand new and horribly unpleasant sensation, and woke up sputtering. It was the scent of ammonia in his nostrils. He woke up sputtering and gagging and bent on mass murder. The first slave he saw, he ordered to kill itself in a horrible manner.

The slave smiled tremulously at him. "Darling, are you all right?" Her voice was terribly strained and her smile was a lie.

Everything came back in a rush. That was Judy . . . "Sure, beautiful, I'm fine. Would you step outside while these good people ask me some questions?"

"Yes, Larry." She stood up and left, hurrying. Kzanol waited until the door was closed before he turned on the others.

"You." He faced the man in the travel chair. He must be in charge; he was obviously the oldest. "Why did you subject Judy to this?"

"I was hoping it would jog your memory. Did it?"

"My memory is perfect. I even remember that Judy is a sentient female, and that the idea of my not being Larry Greenberg would be a considerable shock to her. That's why I sent her away."

"Good for you. Your females aren't sentient?"

"No. It must be strange to have a sentient mate." Kzanol dug momentarily into Greenberg's memories, smiled a dirty smile, then got back to the business at hand. "How did you bring me down?"

The old one shrugged. "Easy enough. We put you to sleep with a sonic, then took over your car's autopilot. The only risk was that you might be on manual. By the way, I'm Garner. That's Masney."

Kzanol took the information without comment. He saw that Masney was a stocky man, so wide that he seemed much shorter than his six feet two inches, and his hair and eating tendrils or whatever were dead white.

Masney was staring thoughtfully at Kzanol. It was the kind of look a new biology student gives a preserved sheep's heart before he goes to work with the scalpel.

"Greenberg," he said, "why'd you do it?"

Kzanol didn't answer.

"Jansky's lost both his eyes and most of his face. Knudsen will be a cripple for nearly a year; you cut his spinal cord. With this." He pulled the disintegrator out of a drawer. "Why? Did you think it would make you king of the world? That's stupid. It's only a hand weapon."

"It's not even that," said Kzanol. He found it easy to speak English. All he had to do was relax. "It's a digging or cutting tool, or a shaping instrument. Nothing more."

Masney stared. "Greenberg," he whispered, as if he were afraid of the answer, "who do you think you are?"

Kzanol tried to tell him. He almost strangled doing it. Overtalk didn't fit human vocal cords. "Not Greenberg," he managed. "Not a . . . slave. Not human."

"Then what?"

He shook his head, rubbing his throat.

"Okay. How does this innocuous tool work?"

"You push that little button and the beam starts removing surface material."

"That's not what I meant."

"Oh. Well, it suppresses the . . . charge on the electron. I think that's right. Then whatever is in the beam starts to tear itself apart. We use the big ones to sculpture mountains." His voice dropped to a whisper. "We did." He started to choke, caught himself. Masney frowned.

Garner asked, "How long were you underwater?"

"I think between one and two billion years. Your years or mine, they aren't that much different."

"Then your race is probably dead."

"Yes." Kzanol looked at his hands, unbelievingly. "How

47

in—" he gurgled, recovered, "how under the Power did I get into this body? Greenberg thought that was only a telepathy machine!"

Garner nodded. "Right. And you've been in that body, so to speak, all along. The alien's memories were superimposed on your brain, Greenberg. You've been doing the same thing with dolphins for years, but it never affected you this way. What's the matter with you, Greenberg? Snap out of it!"

The slave in the travel chair made no move to kill himself. "You," Kzanol/Greenberg paused to translate, "whitefood. You despicable, decaying, crippled whitefood with defective sex organs. Stop telling me who I am! I know who I am!" He looked down at his hands. Tears formed at the corners of his eyes and ran itching down his cheeks, but his face remained as expressionless as a moron's.

Garner blinked at him. "You think you are what's-his-name, the alien terror from Outer Space? Nuts. The alien terror is down on the first floor of this building, and he's perfectly harmless. If we could get him back to normal time he would be the first to call you an impostor. Later I'll take you down and *show* him to you.

"Part of what you said is true. I am, of course, an old man. But what is a, er, whitefood?" He made the word a separate question.

Kzanol had calmed down. "I translated. The whitefood is an artificial animal, created by the tnuctipun as a meat animal. A whitefood is as big as a dinosaur and as smooth and white as a shmoo. They're a lot like shmoos. We can use all of their bodies, except the skeleton, and they eat free food, which is almost as cheap as air. Their shape is like a caterpillar reaching for a leaf. The mouth is at the front of the belly foot."

"Free food?"

Kzanol/Greenberg didn't hear him. "That's funny. Garner, do you remember the pictures of bandersnatchi that the second Jinx expedition sent back? Greenberg

48

was going to read a bandersnatch mind someday."

"Sure. Hey!"

"Bandersnatchi are whitefoods," said Kzanol/Greenberg. "They don't have minds."

"I guessed that. But, son, you've got to remember that they've had two billion years to develop minds."

"It wouldn't help them. They can't mutate. They were designed that way. A whitefood is one big cell, with a chromosome as long as your arm and as thick as your little finger. Radiation could never affect them, and the first thing that would be harmed by any injury would be the budding apparatus." Kzanol/Greenberg was bewildered. What price another coincidence? "Why would anyone think they were intelligent?"

"Well, for one thing," Garner said mildly, "the report said the brain was tremendous. Weighed as much as a three-year-old boy."

Kzanol/Greenberg laughed. "They were designed for that, too. The brain of a whitefood has a wonderful flavor, so the tnuctip engineers increased its size. So?"

"So it's convoluted like a human brain."

Why, so it was. Like a human brain, and a tnuctip brain, and a thrint brain, for that matter. Now why—

Kzanol/Greenberg cracked his knuckles, then hurriedly separated his hands so that he couldn't do it again. The mystery of the intelligent "bandersnatch" bothered him, but he had other things to worry about. Why, for example, hadn't he been rescued? Three hundred years after he pushed the panic button, he must have struck the Earth like the destroying wrath of the Powergiver. Someone on the moon *must* have seen it.

Could the lunar observation post have been abandoned?

Why?

Garner crashed into his thoughts. "Maybe something bigger than a cosmic ray made the mutations. Something like a machine-gun volley or a meteor storm."

49

Kzanol/Greenberg shook his head. "Any other evidence?"

"Oh, hell yes. Greenberg, what do you know about Jinx?"

"A good deal," said Kzanol/Greenberg. Larry's knowledge of Jinx had been as thorough as any colonist's. The memories clicked into place, unbidden, at the sound of the word. Jinx . . .

Moon of Binary, third planet out from Sirius A. Binary was a banded orange giant, bigger than Jupiter, and much warmer. Jinx was six times as big as Earth, with a gravity of one point seven eight, and with a period of rotation more than four days long. Of all the factors which had shaped Jinx, the most important had been its lack of radioactive materials. For Jinx was solid all through its rocky lithosphere and halfway to the center of its nickel-iron core.

Long ago—before even his time, Kzanol's time—Jinx had been much closer to Binary. So close that the tides had stopped her spin and pulled her into an egg shape. Later, those same tides had pushed her outward. Not unusual. But, though the atmosphere and ocean assumed a more spherical shape, Jinx did not. The body of the moon was still egg shaped.

Jinx was an Easter egg, banded in different colors by the varying surface pressures.

The ocean was a broad ring of what must be extremely salty water running through the poles of rotation. The regions which the colonists called the Ends, marked by the points nearest to and furthest from Binary, were six hundred miles "higher" than the ocean: six hundred miles further from the moon's center of mass. They stuck right out of the atmosphere. In the photographs masered in from the first expedition, the Ends had shown bone white, with a tracery of sharp black shadows. Further from the Ends the shadows disappeared beneath the atmosphere, and clouds began to appear. The clouds became thicker and thicker, with brown-and-gray earth showing more and more rarely, until suddenly the clouds were in full control. The ocean was forever hidden beneath a band of permanent fleecy cloud thousands of miles wide. At sea level the air was terrifically dense, with a constant temperature of two hundred and seventy degrees Fahrenheit.

The colony of Sirius Mater was on the Eastern continent, three thousand miles east of the ocean, a triangle of cultivated land and inflatable buildings at the fork of two rivers. The first colonists had picked a landing place with a high surface pressure, knowing that the denser atmosphere would help protect them from the temperature changes during the long days and nights, and from the ultraviolet scourge of blue-white Sirius A. Sirius Mater now boasted a population of almost two hundred punsters of all ages. . . .

"Good," said Garner. "Then I won't have to explain anything. Can I borrow the phone, Lloyd?"

"Sure." Lloyd hooked a thumb at one wall.

The phone screen was a big one; it covered half the wall. Luke dialed thirteen quick motions of the forefinger. In a moment the screen cleared to reveal a slender young woman with wavy brunette hair.

"Technological Police, Records Office."

"This is Lucas Garner, operative-at-large. Here's my ident." He held a plastic card up to the camera. "I'd like the bandersnatchi sections from the Jinx report of 2106."

"Yes sir." The woman rose and walked off camera.

Kzanol/Greenberg leaned forward to watch. The last report from Jinx had arrived only two months ago, and most of it had not been made public. He remembered seeing stills of the bandersnatchi, but no more. Now, with new eyes eager to compare, he would see whether a bandersnatch was really a whitefood.

It should not have mattered. By all rights he should have felt as he had when Masney's sonic sleeping pill first wore off. Friendless, homeless, disembodied, defeated past all hope. But a prisoner's first duty is always to escape: by collaboration, by treachery, by theft and murder, by any means at all. If he could lull these arrogant slaves into thinking he would cooperate, would give information freely—

And he had to know. Later he would decide why the question seemed so important. Now he only knew that it was. The suggestion that a whitefood might be intelligent had hit him with the force of a deadly insult. Why? But never mind why. Was it true?

The girl was back, smiling. "Mr. Garner, I'll now turn you over to Mayor Herkimer." She touched something below the edge of her desk.

The picture dissolved and reformed, but now it was ragged, shot with random dots of colored light. A maser beam had crossed nine light years to bring this picture, and had been somewhat torn up on the way, by dust and gee fields and crossing light waves.

Mayor Herkimer had brown hair and a bushy brown beard over a square jaw. His voice was ragged with interference, but his enunciation was clear and careful—and twisted by an unknown accent.

"—Since everything that wasn't welded down had long since been removed from the Lazy Eight II, and since the fusion plant in the Lazy Eight I was not damaged in the original landing and will give us power for a goddam century, and since there was little work to be done until spring in any case, the Authority voted to risk the Lazy Eight II in exploring Jinx's oceanic regions. Accordingly six of us red-hot explorers, namely—" Herkimer named names, "took the ship up and went west. A circular flying wing isn't exactly a goddam airplane, but the ship was lighter than during first landing, and we had enough power to stay up forever or to make a straight-up landing anywhere we could find flat land.

"One problem was that the goddam visibility kept dropping—"

Garner whispered, "Their slang seems to have changed somewhat since they moved to Jinx."

"Oh, you noticed that?"

Kzanol/Greenberg twitched in annoyance at the interruptions. That would have marked him for an alien anywhere! In 2106 you learned not to hear extraneous noises before you went insane.

"—Couldn't see at all. The light from the fusion drive didn't show us the ground until we were two hundred feet up. We landed on the solid jets, near the shoreline, and started the cameras. Right away we were surrounded by—these."

Mayor Herkimer had a sense of drama. As he stopped talking, the scene jumped to a sandy, sloping beach. The sand in the foreground was blackened and blown into a curving wall. Beyond, the ocean. There were no waves on that ocean. The water seemed—thick. Thick and gray and living.

Something moved into view. Something white; something like an enormously magnified slug, but with a smooth, slick skin. From the front of the beast reared a brontosaur neck with no head at all. At its base the neck was as wide as the animal's shoulders. It rose in a conical slope. The tip was thick and rounded, featureless but for two tufts of black bristles.

The camera watched as the beast approached; saw it stop at the scorched sand. Others of its kind came out of the mist. The camera swept a full circle, and everywhere there were enormous white bulks like albino sperm whales swimming through sand.

Their rounded tips swung back and forth; the tufted bristles blew without wind. Of course the bristles were sense organs; and of course the mouths were invisible because the mouths were all closed. Unusual in a whitefood. But they were whitefoods, and no mistake.

Mayor Herkimer spoke. "These pictures were taken in visible light, but with a long exposure, which accounts for the damn blurring. To us it was like night. Winston

Doheny, our biologist, took one look at these monsters and dubbed them *Frumious bandersnatch*. This species name is now in the goddam log. Harlow went out in a segmented armor suit and shot a bandersnatch for dissection, and the rest ran off. Fortunately the suit stood up to the heat and pressure."

Films showed the action. Tracer bullets stitching six lines from off-camera through the bulky front of a bandersnatch. The silent death, evidenced only by a suddenly drooping tip. White shapes fading ghostlike into the mist. Herkimer continued, "They run on a rippling belly foot, and as you can see, they move goddam fast.

"According to Doheny this animal is one big cell. Nerves are similar to human nerves in structure, but have no cell body, no nuclei, nothing to separate them from other specialized protoplasm. The brain is long and narrow, and is packed into a bone shell at the elevated tapering tip. This skull is one end of a jointless, flexible, very strong internal cage of bone. Apparently God never intended the beast to shift position." Garner winced at the unconscious blasphemy. "The mouth, which was closed in the film, is just ahead of the belly foot, and is good for nothing but scooping up yeast from the ocean."

The film showed details from the dissection of the bandersnatch. Evidently the two cops at the door had decided not to look; but Masney and Garner watched in keen interest. Autopsies were nothing new to them. The beast was turned on its side to expose the belly foot, and its jaws were opened with a pulley. Slides were shown of tissue sections. There was a circulatory system, with six hearts weighing eleven pounds apiece; there were strange organs in the left side, which only Kzanol/ Greenberg recognized as budding apparatus. He watched with manic concentration as the brain case was opened to show the long, narrow brain, gray and deeply convoluted, in its canoe of a skull. The form was familiar in detail, though he'd never seen one raw. Then it was over, and Mayor Herkimer was back.

"The ocean is a uniform foot thick in some unknown breed of yeast. Herds of bandersnatchi move along the shoreline, feeding continuously. The shore is no goddam tourist trap. It's always dark, the waves are smothered by the yeast and the gravity, and the bandersnatchi wander along the shore like the lost souls of worn-away mountains. We'd have liked to leave right then, but Doheny couldn't find the sex organs, and he wanted to make a few more dissections.

"So we sent out the copters to find another specimen. But no bandersnatch ever came close enough to be shot from a copter. The bandersnatchi had been curious and unafraid. Now they ran whenever a copter got close. All of them. They couldn't possibly have all known about us, unless they were either telepathic or had a language.

"Yet at least one goddam bandersnatch was always within sight of each copter. They seemed to know the range of our guns.

"On the third day of the hunt Doheny got impatient. He assumed that it was the copters that the bandersnatchi were afraid of, and he landed his goddam copter and went hunting on foot. The moment he was out of shooting range of the copter, a bandersnatch charged in and flattened it like a goddam freight truck running down a pedestrian. Doheny had to walk back.

"Several hundred miles east of the shore, we found other forms of native—"

Mayor Herkimer was cut off in midsentence. The slender brunette's voice came from a blank screen: "Mr. Garner, there is another section of the report listed under 'bandersnatchi.' Do you want it?"

"Yes, but just a minute." Garner turned to face Kzanol/Greenberg. "Greenberg, were those white-foods?"

"Yes."

"Are they telepathic?"

"No. And I've never heard of them avoiding a meat packer's ship. They just go on eating until they're dead."

"Okay, miss, we're ready."

Again there was the square, bearded face of the mayor. "We returned to Sirius Mater five Jinx days after our departure. We found that *Frumious bandersnatch* had preceded us. A single specimen. It must have traveled three thousand miles without yeast, and without any other food source that it could use, just to visit our settlement. To do this it must have gorged itself for months, maybe years, in order to build up enough fat for the trip.

"The colonists let it alone, which was goddam sensible of them, and the bandersnatch didn't come too close. By this time its skin, or its cell wall, was light blue, possibly for protection from sunlight. It went straight to Northwest Cultivation Area, spent two hours running tracks across it in what Vicemayor Tays claims was the damnedest dance he ever saw, then moved off toward the ocean.

"Since we had both copters, we were the first to see the tracks from above. These are films of the tracks. I am convinced that this is a form of writing. Doheny says it can't be. He believes that a bandersnatch could have no use for intelligence, hence would not develop it. I have to admit the sonofabitch has a good argument. The bandersnatch makes a beached dolphin look like a miracle of dexterity. Would you please analyze this and let us know whether we share this world with an intelligent species?"

"The machines couldn't make anything out of this," Garner put in. "Concepts were too alien, maybe."

From the phone screen came kaleidoscopic color static, then a fuzzy picture. Curved lines, like snail tracks, on brown earth. The earth was plowed in mathematically straight furrows, but the lines were broader and deeper. Hillocks and tree stumps distorted them. A

56

helicopter had landed among the wavy tracks; it looked like a fly on a printed page.

Kzanol/Greenberg choked, gurgled, and said, " 'Leave our planet at once or be obliterated, in accordance with the treaty of—' I can't read the rest. But it's tnuctip science language. Could I have some water?"

"Sure," Masney said kindly. He jerked a thumb at the cooler. After a moment Kzanol/Greenberg got up and poured his own water.

Lloyd went over to Garner's chair and began talking in a low voice. "Luke, what was that all about? What are you doing?"

"Just satisfying curiosity. Relax, Lloyd. Dr. Snyder will be here in an hour, then he can take over. Meanwhile there are a lot of things Greenberg can tell us. This isn't just a man with hallucinations, Lloyd.

"Why would the ET's race have thought that the bandersnatch was just a dumb animal? Why does he react so violently when we suggest that the thing might be sentient? Greenberg thinks he's the prisoner of aliens, he thinks his race is billions of years dead and his home lost forever, yet what is it that really interests him? *Frumious bandersnatch.* Did you see the way he looked when the dissection was going on?"

"No. I was too interested myself."

"I get almost scared when I think of what's in Greenberg's brain—the information he's carrying. Do you realize that Dr. Snyder may have to permanently repress those memories to cure him?

"Why would a race as sophisticated as the tnuctipun must have been"—he pronounced the word as Kzanol/ Greenberg had, badly—"have worked for Greenberg's adapted race? Was it because of the telepathy? I'm just—"

"I can tell you that," Kzanol/Greenberg said bitterly. He had drunk five cups of water, practically without a breath. Now he was panting a little.

"You've got good ears," said Masney.

"No. I'm a little telepathic; just enough to get by on. It's Greenberg's talent, but he didn't really believe in it so he couldn't use it. I can. Much good may it do me."

"So why did the tnuctipun work for you?" Masney messed up the word even worse than Garner had.

The question answered itself.

Everyone in the room jerked like hooked fish.

There was no fall. An instant after he put out his arms, Kzanol was resting on his six fingertips like a man doing pushups. He stayed there a moment, then got to his feet. The gravity was a little heavy.

Where was everybody? Where was the thrint or slave who had released him?

He was in an empty, hideously alien building, the kind that happen only on free slave worlds before the caretakers move in. But . . . how had he gotten here, when he was aimed at a deserted food planet? The next sight he had expected was the inside of a caretaker's palace. And where was everybody? He badly needed someone to tell him what was going on.

He Listened.

For some reason, neither human nor thrintun beings have flaps over their ears resembling the flaps over their eyes. The thrintun Power faculty is better protected. Kzanol was not forced to lower his mental shield all at once. He chose to do so, and he paid for it. It was like looking into an arc lamp from a foot away. Nowhere in the thrintun universe would the telepathic noise have been that intense. The slave worlds never held this heavy an overpopulation; and the teeming masses of the thrintun worlds kept their mind shields up in public.

Kzanol reeled from the pain. His reaction was immediate and automatic.

STOP THINKING AT ME! he roared at the bellowing minds of Topeka, Kansas.

In the complex of mental hospitals still called Menninger's, thousands of doctors and nurses and patients heard the command. Hundreds of patients eagerly took it as literal and permanent. Some became stupid and cured. Others went catatonic. A few who had been harmlessly irresponsible became dangerously so. A handful of doctors became patients, a mere handful, but the loss of their services compounded the emergency when the casualties began pouring in from downtown. Menninger's was miles from Topeka Police Headquarters.

In the little room, everyone jerked like hooked fish. Then, all but Kzanol/Greenberg, they stopped moving. Their faces were empty. They were idiots.

In the first instant of the mental blast, Kzanol/Greenberg's mental shield went up with an almost audible clang. A roaring noise reverberated through his mind for minutes. When he could think again, he still didn't dare drop the mind shield.

There was a thrint on Earth.

The guards at the door now squatted or sat like rag dolls. Kzanol/Greenberg pulled cigarettes from a dark blue shirt pocket and lit one from the burning butt between Masney's lips, incidentally saving Masney a nasty burn. He sat and smoked while he thought about the other thrint.

Item: That thrint would see him as a slave.

Item: He, Kzanol, had a working mind shield. That might convince the thrint, whoever he was, that he, Kzanol, was a thrint in a human body. Or it might not. If it did, would the other thrint help? Or would he re-

59

gard Kzanol/Greenberg as a mere ptavv, a Powerless thrint?

In ugly fact, Kzanol/Greenberg *was* a ptavv. He had to get his body back before the other found him.

And with that, incredibly, he stopped thinking about the other thrint. There was every reason to wonder about him. What was he doing on Earth? Would he claim Earth as his property? Would he help Kzanol/Greenberg reach Thrintun (or whatever new planet passed for Thrintun these days)? Did he still look thrintish, or had two billion years of evolution turned thrintun into monsters? But Kzanol/Greenberg dropped the subject and began to think about reaching Neptune. Perhaps he knew who the other thrint was, but wasn't ready to face the fact.

Cautiously he Listened. The thrint had left the building. He could find out nothing more, for the other's mind shield was up. He turned his Attention, such as it was, to the men in the room.

They were recovering, but very slowly. He had to Listen with excruciating concentration because of the limitations of Greenberg's brain, but he could feel their personalities reintegrating. The most advanced seemed to be Garner. Next was Masney.

Another part of the Greenberg memory was about to become useful. Greenberg had not lied about his dolphin-like sense of the practical joke. To implement it he had spent weeks learning a technique for what we shall charitably call a party trick.

Kzanol/Greenberg bent over Lloyd Masney. "Lloyd," he said, in a distinct, calm, authoritative voice. "Concentrate on the sound of my voice. You will hear only the sound of my voice. Your eyelids are getting heavy. So heavy. Your fingers are becoming tired. So tired. Let them go limp. Your eyes wish to close; you can hardly keep them open . . ."

He could feel the Masney personality responding beautifully. It gave no resistance at all.

The gravity was irritating. It was barely enough to notice at first, but after a few minutes it was exhausting. Kzanol gave up the idea of walking after he had gone less than a block, though he didn't like the idea of riding in a slave cart.

I'm not proud, he told himself. He climbed into a parked Cadillac and ordered the slack-lipped driver to take him to the nearest spaceport. There was a fang-jarring vibration, and the car took off with a wholly unnecessary jerk.

These slaves were much larger than the average land-bound sentient being. Kzanol had plenty of head room. After a moment he cautiously took off his helmet. The air was a little thin, which was puzzling considering the heavy gravity. Otherwise it was good enough. He dropped the helmet on the seat and swung his legs over beside it; the seat was too wide for comfort.

The city was amazing. Huge and grotesque! The eye was faced with nothing but rectangular prisms, with here and there a yellow rectangular field or a flattish building with a strangely curved roof. The streets couldn't decide whether to be crooked or straight. Cars zipped by, buzzing like flying pests. The drone from the fans of his own car rasped on his nerves, until he learned to ignore it.

But where was he? He must have missed F124 somehow, and hit here. The driver knew that his planet—Earth?—had space travel, and therefore might know how to find F124. And the eighth planet of its system.

For it was already obvious that he would need the second suit. These slaves outnumbered him seventeen billion to one. They could destroy him at any time. And would, when they knew what he was. He had to get the control helmet to make himself safe. Then he would have to find a thrintun planet; and he might need a better spaceship than the humans had produced so far. They must be made to produce better ships.

The buildings were getting lower, and there were even

61

gaps between them. Had poor transportation made these slaves crowd together in clumps? Someday he must spend the time to find out more about them. After all, they were his now.

But what a story this would make someday! How his grandchildren would listen and admire! When the time came he must buy balladeers; pruntaquilun balladeers, for only these had the proper gift of language . . .

The spaceport was drawing near.

There was no apparent need to be subtle. Once Kzanol/Greenberg had Masney fully under, he simply ordered Masney to take him to the spaceport. It took about fifteen minutes to reach the gate.

At first he couldn't guess why Masney was landing. Shouldn't he simply fly over the fence? Masney wasn't giving away information. His mind would have been nearly normal by now, and it was normal for a hypnotized person. Masney "knew" that he wasn't really hypnotized; he was only going along with it for a joke. Any time now he would snap out of it and surprise Greenberg. Meanwhile he was calm and happy and free from the necessity for making decisions. He had been told to go to the spaceport. Here he was at the spaceport. His passenger let him lead.

Not until they were down did Kzanol/Greenberg realize that Masney was waiting to be passed through by the guards. He asked, "Will the guards let us through?"

"No," said Masney.

Coosth, another setback. "Would they have let me through with—" he thought, "Garner?"

"Yes. Garner's an Arm."

"Well, turn around and go back for Garner."

The car whirred. "Wait a minute," said Kzanol/Greenberg. "Sleep." Where were the guards?

Across a tremendous flat expanse of concrete, painted with large red targets in a hexagonal array, he could see the spaceships. There were twenty or thirty ramjet-rocket orbital craft, some fitted out to lift other space-craft to orbit. A linear accelerator ran down the entire south side of the field: a quarter mile of wide, closely set metal hoops. Fusion-drive military rockets lay on their sides in docks, ready to be loaded onto the flat triangular ramjet-rockets. They all looked like motor scooters beside two truly gigantic craft.

One thing like a monstrous tin of tuna, a circular fly-ing wing resting on its blunt trailing edge, was the re-entry, cargo, and life-support system of the Lazy Eight III. Anyone would have recognized her, even without the blue human's sign of infinity on her flank. She was 320 feet in diameter, 360 in height. The other, far to the right, was a passenger ship as big as the ancient *Queen Mary,* one of the twin luxury transports which served the Titan Hotel. And—even at this distance it was apparent that everybody, *everybody* was clustered around her entrance port.

Listening as hard as he could, Kzanol/Greenberg still couldn't find out what they were doing there; but he rec-ognized the flavor of those far-too-calm thoughts. Those were tame slaves, slaves under orders.

The other thrint was here. But why wasn't he taking his own ship? Or had he landed here? Or—was the spawn of a ptavv making a leisurely inspection of his new property?

He told Masney, "The guard has told us to go ahead. Take the car over to that honeymoon special."

The car skimmed across the concrete.

Garner shook his head, let it fall back into place. His mind was as the mind of a sleeping child. Across that mind flitted thoughts as ephemeral as dreams. They could not stay. Garner had been ordered not to think.

I must look terribly senile, he thought once. The idea slipped away . . . and returned. Senile. I'm old but not senile. No? There is drool on my chin.

He shook his head, hard. He slapped his face with one

63

hand. Garner was beginning to think again, but not fast enough to suit him. He fumbled at the controls of his chair, and it lurched over to the coffee faucet. When he poured a cup his hand shook so that hot coffee spilled on his hand and wrist. Enraged, he hurled the cup at the wall.

His mind went back to white dullness.

A few minutes later Judy Greenberg wobbled through the door. She looked dazed, but her mind was functioning again. She saw Garner slumped in his travel chair wearing the face of a decrepit moron, and she poured cold water over his head until he came to life.

"Where is he?" Garner demanded.

"I don't know," Judy told him. "I saw him walk out, but it didn't seem to matter to me. Chief Masney was with him. What happened to us?"

"Something I should have expected." Garner was no longer a decrepit old man, but an angry Jehovah. "It means things have gone from worse to terrible. That alien statue—I knew there was something wrong with it the moment I saw it, but I couldn't see what it was. Oh, nuts.

"It had both arms out, like it was turning chicken halfway through a swan dive. I saw a little projection on his chest, too. Look. The alien put himself into a freeze field to avoid some disaster. After that the button that turned on the field was in the field, and so was the alien's finger pushing it in. So the button wouldn't need a catch to hold it in. It wouldn't have one.

"But the alien had both arms out when I saw it. When Jansky put his own field around the statue, the alien dropped Greenberg's 'digging instrument' and the button too. The button must have popped out. Why he didn't come to life right then I don't know, unless the freeze field has inertia like hysteresis in an electric current. But he's alive now, and that was him we heard."

"Well, it's quite a monster," said Judy. "Is that what Larry thinks he is?"

"Right." Garner's chair rose and made a wind in the room. The chair slid out the door, picking up speed. Judy stared after it.

"Then if he sees that he isn't who he thinks he is . . ." she began hopefully. Then she gave it up.

One of the policemen got to his feet, moving like a sleepwalker.

Kzanol took the guards with him on his tour of the spaceport. He also took all the repairmen, dispatchers, spacemen, and even passengers he happened to meet while moving around. The man who owned the Cadillac seemed to regard even a trip to Mars as a hazardous journey! If that was the state of Earth's space technology, Kzanol wanted a bundleful of expert opinions.

A couple of dispatchers were sent back to the office to try to find F124 on the star maps. The rest of the group came with Kzanol, growing as it moved. Just two men had the sense to hide when they saw the mob coming. By the time he reached the passenger liner Kzanol was towing everyone at the spaceport but Masney, Kzanol/ Greenberg, and those two cautious men.

He had already chosen the Lazy Eight III, the only interstellar ship on the field. While he was getting the rescue switch on his back repaired, slaves could finish building and orbiting the ship's drive and fuel tanks. It would be at least a year before he was ready to leave Earth. Then he would take a large crew and pass the journey in stasis, with his slaves to wake him whenever a new child became old enough to take orders. Their descendants would wake him at journey's end.

Kzanol had stood beneath the blunt ring which was the

ship's trailing edge and looked up into the gaping mouth of a solid fuel landing motor. He had probed an engineer's mind to find how the spin of a ship could substitute for artificial gravity. He had walked on the after wall of the central corridor and peered through doors above his head and beneath his feet, into the Garden whose rows of hydroponic tanks served in place of his own tnuctip-bred air plant, and into the huge control room with three walls covered in nightmare profusion with dials and screens and switchboards. His own ship had needed only a screen and a brain board. Everywhere he saw ingenuity replacing true knowledge, complex makeshifts replacing the compact, simple machines Kzanol had known. Dared he trust his life to this jury-rigged monster?

He had no choice. The remarkable thing was that humans would do so; that they would scheme and fight to do so. The space urge was a madness upon them— a madness which should be cured quickly, lest they waste this world's resources.

This prospecting trip, Kzanol thought wryly, is taking longer than I dreamed. And then, not at all wryly: Will I ever see Thrintun again?

Well, at least he had time to burn. As long as he was here, he might as well see what a human called a luxury liner.

He was impressed despite himself.

There were thrintun liners bigger than the *Golden Circle,* and a few which were far bigger; but not many carried a greater air of luxury. Those that did carried the owners of planets. The ramjets under the triangular wing were almost as big as some of the military ships on the field. The builders of the *Golden Circle* had cut corners only where they wouldn't show. The lounge looked huge, much bigger than it actually was. It was paneled in gold and navy blue. Crash couches folded into the wall to give way to a bar, a small dance floor, a compact casino. Dining tables rose neatly and automatically from the carpeted floor, inverting themselves to show dark-grained plastic-oak. The front wall was a giant tri-dee screen. When the water level in the fuel tanks became low enough, an entrance from the lounge turned the tank into a swimming pool. Kzanol was puzzled by the layout until he realized that the fusion drive was in the belly. Ramjets would lift the ship to a safe altitude, but from then on the fusion drive would send thrust up instead of forward. The ship used water instead of liquid hydrogen, not because the passengers needed a pool, but because water was safer to carry and provided a reserve oxygen supply. The staterooms were miracles of miniaturization.

There were, thought Kzanol, ideas here that he could use when he got back to civilization. He sat down in one of the lounge crash couches and began leafing through some of the literature stuffed into the backs. One of the first things he found, of course, was a beautifully colored picture of Saturn as seen from the main dance bubble of the Titan Hotel.

Of course he recognized it. He began to ask eager questions of the men around him.

The truth hit him all at once.

Kzanol/Greenberg gasped, and his shield went up with a clang. Masney wasn't so fortunate. He shrieked and clutched his head, and shrieked again. In Topeka, thirty miles away, unusually sensitive people heard the scream of rage and grief and desolation.

At Menninger's, a girl who had been catatonic for four years forced doughy leg muscles to hold her erect while she looked around her. Someone needed help; someone needed her.

Lucas Garner gasped and stopped his chair with a jerk. Alone among the pedestrians around him, who were behaving as if they had very bad headaches, Garner listened. There must be information buried in all that emotion! But Garner learned nothing. He felt the sense of

67

loss becoming his own, sapping his will to live until he felt he was drowning in a black tide.

"It doesn't hurt," said Kzanol/Greenberg in a calm, reassuring, very loud voice. The loudness, hopefully, would carry over Masney's screaming. "You can feel it but it doesn't hurt. Anyway, you have enormous courage, more than you have ever had in your whole life." Masney stopped screaming, but his face was a mask of suffering. "All right," said Kzanol/Greenberg. "Sleep." He brushed Masney's face with his fingertips. Masney collapsed. The car continued weightlessly across the concrete, riding its cushion of air, aiming itself at the cylindrical shell that was the Lazy Eight III. Kzanol/Greenberg let it go. He couldn't operate the controls from the back seat, and Masney was in no shape to help. He could have cut the air cushion, by stretching, but only if he wanted to die.

The mental scream ended. He put his hand on Masney's shoulder and said, "Stop the car, Lloyd." Masney took over with no sign, physical or mental, of panic. The car dropped gently to the ground two yards from the outer hull of the giant colony ship.

"Sleep," said Kzanol/Greenberg, and Masney slept. It would probably do him good. He was still under hypnosis, and would be deeper when he awakened. As for Kzanol/Greenberg, he didn't know what he wanted. To rest and think perhaps. Food wouldn't hurt him either, he decided. He had recognized the mind that screamed its pain over half of Kansas, and he needed time to know that he was not Kzanol, thrint, lord of creation.

By and by there was a roar like a fusor exploding. Kzanol/Greenberg saw a wave of flaming smoke pour across the concrete, then gradually diminish. He couldn't imagine what it was. Cautiously he lowered his mind shield and found out.

Jato units. Kzanol was going after the second suit.

Ships and scopes and Confinement Asteroid—by these you may measure the Belt.

A century ago, when the Belt was first being settled, the ships used ion drives and fission batteries and re-starting chemical attitude jets. Now they use fusion tubes, based on a method of forcing the inner surface of a crystal-zinc tube to reflect most forms of energy and matter. The compact air converter has replaced tanked air and hydroponics, at least for months-long hops, though the interstellar colony ships must grow plants for food. Ships have become smaller, more dependable, more versatile, cheaper, far faster, and infinitely more numerous. There are tens of thousands of ships in the Belt.

But there are millions of telescopes. Every ship carries at least one. Telescopes in the Trojan asteroids watch the stars, and Earth buys the films with seeds and water and manufactured products, since Earth's telescopes are too near the Sun to avoid distortion by gravity bend and solar wind. Telescopes watch Earth and Moon, and these films are secret. Telescopes watch each other, re-computing the orbit of each important asteroid as the planets pull it from its course.

Confinement Asteroid is unique.

Early explorers had run across a roughly cylindrical block of solid nickel-iron two miles long by a mile thick, orbiting not far from Ceres. They had marked its path and dubbed it S-2376.

Those who came sixty years ago were workmen with a plan. They drilled a hole down the asteroid's axis, filled it with plastic bags of water, and closed both ends. Solid fuel jets spun S-2376 on its axis. As it spun, solar mirrors bathed it in light, slowly melted it from the surface to the center. When the water finished exploding, and the rock had cooled, the workmen had a cylindrical nickel-iron bubble twelve miles long by six in diameter.

It had been expensive already. Now it was more so. They rotated the bubble to provide half a gee of gravity, filled it with air and with tons of expensive water, covered the interior with a mixture of pulverized stony meteorite material and garbage seeded with select bacteria. A fusion tube was run down the axis, three miles up from everywhere: a very special fusion tube, made permeable to certain wavelengths of light. A gentle bulge in the middle created the wedding-ring lake which now girdles the little inside-out world. Sunshades a mile across were set to guard the poles from light, so that snow could condense there, fall of its own weight, melt, and run in rivers to the lake.

The project took a quarter of a century to complete.

Thirty-five years ago Confinement freed the Belt of its most important tie to Earth. Women cannot have children in free fall. Confinement, with two hundred square miles of usable land, could house one hundred thousand in comfort; and one day it will. But the population of the Belt is only eight hundred thousand; Confinement's score hovers around twenty thousand, mostly women, mostly transient, mostly pregnant.

Lars held a raw carrot in one hand and the knob of a film scanner in the other. He was running six hours of film through the machine at a rate which would have finished the roll in fifteen minutes. The film had been taken through one of the Eros cameras, all of which now pointed at Earth.

For most of the next week, Eros would be the closest asteroid to Earth. The films would be running constantly.

Suddenly Lars stopped chewing. His hand moved. The film ran back a little. Stopped.

There it was. One frame was whited out almost to the corners.

Lars moved the film to a larger scanner and began running it through, slowly, starting several frames back. Twice he used the magnifying adjustment. Finally he muttered, "Idiots."

He crossed the room and began trying to find Ceres with a maser.

70

The duty man picked up the earphones with his usual air of weary patience. He listened silently, knowing that the source was light-minutes away. When the message began to repeat he thumbed a button and said, "Jerry, find Eros and send the following. Recording. Thank you, Eros, your message received in full. We'll get right on it, Lars. Now I've got news for you." The man's colorless voice took on a note of relish. "From Tanya. The 'doc says in seven months you'll be the father of healthy twin girls. Repeat, twin girls . . ."

Carefully, with a constant tapping of fingers on attitude jet buttons, Lit Shaeffer brought his ship into dock at Confinement's pole. A constant thirty miles below, Ceres was a pitted boulder spotted with glassy-looking bubbles of flexible transparent plastic. He rested for a little—docking was always tricky, and Confinement's rotation was unsettling even at the axis—then climbed out the lock and jumped. He landed in the net above the nearest of the ten personnel airlocks. Like a spider on a web, he climbed down to the steel door and crawled in. Ten minutes later, after passing through twelve more doors, he reached the locker room.

A mark piece rented him a locker and he stowed his suit and jet pack inside, revealing himself as a scrawny giant with dark, curly hair and a mahogany tan confined strictly to his face and hands. He bought a paper coverall from a dispenser. Lit and Marda were among the several hundred Belters who did not become nudists in a shirtsleeve environment. It marked them as kooks, which was not a bad thing in the Belt.

The last door let him out behind the heat shield, still in free fall. A spring lift took him four miles down to where he could get a tricycle motor scooter. Even Belters couldn't keep a two-wheeler upright against Confinement's shifting Coriolis force. The scooter took him down a steep gradient which leveled off into plowed fields, greenhouses, toiling farm machinery, woods and streams and scattered cottages. In ten minutes he was home.

No, not really home. The cottage was rented from what there was of a Belt government. A Belter's home is the interior of his suit. But with Marda waiting inside, dark and big-boned and just beginning to show her pregnancy, it felt like homecoming.

Then Lit remembered the coming fight. He hesitated a moment, consciously relaxing, before he rang.

The door disappeared, zzzip. They stood facing each other.

"Lit," said Marda, flatly, as if there was no surprise at all. Then, "There's a call for you."

"I'll take care of that first."

In the Belt as on Earth, privacy was rare and precious. The phone booth was a transparent prism, soundproof. Lit sneaked a last look at Marda before he answered the call. She looked both worried and determined.

"Hello, Cutter. What's new?"

"Hello, Lit. That's why I'm calling," said the duty man at Ceres. Cutter's voice was colorless as always. So was his appearance. Cutter would have looked appropriate dispensing tickets or stamps from behind a barred window. "Lars Stiller just called. One of the honeymoon specials to Titan just took off without calling us. Any comments?"

"Comments? Those stupid, bubbleheaded—" The traffic problem in space was far more than a matter of colliding spacecraft. No two spacecraft had ever collided, but men had died when their ships went through the exhaust of a fusion motor. Telescopic traffic checks, radio transmissions, rescue missions, star and asteroid observations could all be thrown out of whack by a jaywalker.

"That's what *I* said, Lit. What'll we do, turn 'em back?"

"Oh, Cutter, why don't you go to Earth and start your own government?" Lit rubbed his temples hard with both

72

hands, rubbing away the tension. "Sorry. I shouldn't have said that. Marda's having trouble, and it's bugging me. But how can we turn back thirty honeymooning flatlanders, each a multimillionaire? Things are tense enough now. Want to start the Last War?"

"I guess not. Sorry to hear about Marda. What's wrong?"

"She didn't get here in time. The baby's growing too fast."

"That's a damn shame."

"Yeah."

"What about the honeymooner?"

Lit turned his thoughts away from the coming storm. "Assign somebody to watch her and broadcast her course. Then write up a healthy bill for the service and send it to Titan Enterprises, Earth. If it isn't paid in two weeks we send a copy to the UN and demand action."

"Figures. 'Bye, Lit."

Conceived in free fall, gestated in free fall for almost three months, the child was growing too fast. The question could smash a marriage: Let the 'doc abort now? Or wait, slow the child's growth with the appropriate hormone injections, and hope that it wouldn't be born a monster?

But there was no such hope.

Lit felt like he was drowning. With a terrible effort he kept his voice gentle. "There'll be other children, Marda."

"But will there? It's so risky, hoping I can get to Confinement before it's too late. Oh, Lit, let's wait until we're *sure*."

She'd waited three months between 'doc checks! But Lit couldn't say so now, or ever. Instead he said, "Marda, the autodoc is sure, and Dr. Siropopolous is sure. I'll tell you what I've been thinking. We could take a house right here in Confinement until you're pregnant again. It's been done before. Granted it's expensive—"

The phone rang.

73

"Yes?" he barked. "Cutter, what's wrong now?"

"Two things. Brace yourself."

"Go ahead."

"One. The honeymooner is not going to Titan. It seems to be headed in the direction of Neptune."

"But— Better give me the rest of it."

"A military ship just took off from Topeka Base. It's chasing the honeymooner, and they didn't call us this time either!"

"That's more than peculiar. How long is the honeymooner on its way?"

"An hour and a half. No turnover yet, but of course it could be headed for any number of asteroids."

"Oh, that's just great." Lit closed his eyes for a moment. "It almost sounds like something's wrong with the honeymooner, and the other ship's trying a rescue mission. Could something have blown in the life-support system?"

"I'd guess not, not in the *Golden Circle*. Honeymooners have fail-safe on their fail-safe. But you'd better hear the punch line."

"Fire."

"The military ship took off from the field on its fusion drive."

"Then—" There was only one conceivable answer. Lit began to laugh. "Somebody stole it!"

Cutter smiled thinly. "Exactly. Once again, shall we turn either of them back?"

"Certainly not. For one thing, if we threaten to shoot we may have to do it. For another, Earth is very touchy about what rights they have in space. For a third, this is their problem, and their ships. For a fourth, I want to see what happens. Don't you get it yet, Cutter?"

"My guess is that both ships have been stolen." Cutter was still smiling.

"No, no. Too improbable. The military ship was stolen, but the honeymooner must have been sabotaged. We're about to witness the first case of space piracy!"

"O-o-oh. Fifteen couples, and all their jewels, plus, uh,

ransom—you know, I believe you're right!" And Lit Shaeffer was the first man in years to hear Cutter laugh in public.

～※～

In the dead of August the Kansas countryside was a steam bath with sunlamps. Under the city's temperature umbrella it was a cool, somewhat breezy autumn, but the air hit Luke Garner like the breath of Hell as his chair shot through the intangible barrier between Cool and Hot. From there he traveled at top speed, not much caring if his chair broke down as long as he could get into an air conditioned hospital.

He stopped at the spaceport checkpoint, was cleared immediately, and crossed the concrete like a ram on a catapult. The hospital stood like a wedge of Swiss cheese at the edge of the vast landing field, its sharp corner pointed inward. He got inside before heat stroke could claim him.

The line before the elevator was discouragingly long. His chair was rather bulky; he would need an elevator almost to himself. And people were no longer over-polite to their elders. There were too many elders around these days. Garner inhaled deeply of cool air, then went back out.

Outside the doors he fumbled in the ashtray on the left arm of his chair. The motor's purr rose to a howl, and suddenly it wasn't a ground-effect motor any more. If Masney could see him now! Six years ago Masney had profanely ordered him to get rid of the illegal power booster or be run in for using a manually operated flying vehicle. Anything for a friend, Luke had reasoned, and had hidden the control in the ashtray.

The ground dwindled. The edge of the building shot downward past him: sixty stories of it. Now he could see the scars left by Greenberg and Masney. The wavering fusion flame had splashed molten concrete in all directions, had left large craters and intricate earthworm-track runnels, had crossed the entrance to a passenger tunnel and left molten metal pouring down the stairs. Men and machines were at work cleaning up the mess.

The sun deck was below him. Luke brought the travel chair down on the roof and scooted past startled sunbathing patients and into the elevator.

Going down it was dead empty. He got out on the fifty-second floor and showed his credentials to a nurse.

They were all in one ward. Miday, Sandler, Buzin, Katz —there were twenty-eight of them, the men who had been closest to Kzanol when he threw his tantrum. Seven were buried in plastic cocoons. The alien had forgotten to order them to cover, and they had been in the way of the blast when the *Golden Circle* took off. The others were under sleep-inducers. Their faces twisted sometimes with the violence of their dreams.

"I'm Jim Skarwold," said a blond, chubby man in an intern's uniform. "I've heard of you, Mr. Garner. Is there anything I can do for you?"

"There better be." Garner sent his glance down the line of treatment tanks. "Can any of these men stand a dose of scopolamine? They may have information I need."

"Scop? I don't think so. Mr. Garner, what happened to them? I took some psychiatry in college, but I never heard of anything like this. It isn't withdrawal from reality, it isn't straight or crooked fear. . . . They're in despair, but not like other people.

"I was told they got this way from contact with an ET. If you could tell me more about it, I'd have a better chance of treating them."

"Right. Here's what I know," said Garner. He told the doctor everything that had happened since the statue

76

was retrieved from the ocean. The doctor listened in silence.

"Then it isn't just a telepath," he said when Garner finished. "It can control minds. But what could it have ordered them to do that would produce *this*?" He gestured at the row of sleeping patients.

"Nothing. I don't think he was giving orders at the time. He just got a helluva shock and started feeling out loud." Luke dropped a huge hand on the doctor's shoulder, and Skarwold twitched his surprise at the weight. "Now, if I were planning to treat them, I'd find out first who they think they are. Themselves? Or the alien? The ET may have superimposed his own emotional pattern on theirs, or even his memory pattern.

"Being me, and an Arm, I want to know why both Greenberg and the ET separately stole spaceships and went rocketing off. They must know they've got interplanetary ships, not interstellar colony craft. Is there an alien base somewhere in the solar stystem? What are they after?

"Perhaps we can scratch both problems at the same time, Dr. Skarwold."

"Yes," said Skarwold slowly. "Perhaps you're right. Give me an hour to find the man with the strongest heart."

That was why Luke always carried paperbacks in the glove compartment of his chair. His career involved a lot of waiting.

Arthur T. Katz, qualified ramjet-rocket booster pilot (types C, D, and H-1), thrashed violently. His arms flailed without purpose. He began to make noises.

"It'll be a few minutes," said Skarwold. "He's out of the sleep-inducer, but he has to wake up naturally."

Garner nodded. He was studying the man intently, with his eyes narrowed and his lips tightened slightly. He might have been watching a strange dog, wondering whether it wanted to lick his face or tear his throat out.

Katz opened his eyes. They became very round, then closed desperately tight. Cautiously Katz opened them again. He screamed and waved his arms meaninglessly in the air. Then he started to choke. It was horrible to watch. Whenever he somehow managed to catch his breath he would gasp for air for a few seconds, open his mouth, and begin to choke again. He was terrified, and, thought Garner, not merely because he might suffocate.

Skarwold pushed a switch and Katz's autodoc sprayed sedative into his lungs. Katz flopped back and began to breathe deeply. Skarwold turned on Katz's sleep-inducer.

Abruptly Garner asked, "Are any of these people the least bit psychic?"

Arnold Diller, fusion drive inspector (all conventional types), took a deep breath and began turning his head back and forth. Not gently. It seemed he was trying to break his own neck.

"I wish we could have found someone with a high telepathic aptitude," said Garner. Between the palms of his hands he rolled the sawdust fragments of a cigarette. "He would have stood a better chance. Look at the poor guy!"

Skarwold said, "I think he's got a good chance."

Garner shook his head. "He's only a poor man's prescient. If he were any good at that he'd have been running instead of hiding when the ET blew up. How could it protect him against telepathy anyway? He—"

Skarwold joggled his arm for silence.

"Diller!" said Skarwold, with authority. Diller stopped tossing his head and looked up. "Can you understand me, Diller?"

Diller opened his mouth and started to strangle. He closed it again, and nodded, breathing through his nose.

"My name is Skarwold, and I'm your doctor." He paused as if in doubt. "You *are* Arnold Diller, aren't you?"

"Yes." The voice was rusty, hesitant, as if from long disuse. Something inside Garner relaxed, and he noticed his handful of sawdust and dropped it.

"How do you feel?"

"Terrible. I keep wanting to breathe wrong, talk wrong. Could I have a cigarette?" Garner handed him a lighted one. Diller's voice began to sound better, more proficient. "That was strange. I tried to *make* you give me a cigarette. When you just sat there I wanted to get mad." He frowned. "Say, how do I rate a human doctor, anyway?"

"What happened to you isn't programmed into the 'docs," Skarwold said lightly. "It's a good thing you had the sense to hide when you did. The others were closer. They're in much worse shape. Is your prescient sense working?"

"It's not telling me anything. I can never count on it anyway. Why?"

"Well, that's why I picked you. I thought if you missed it you could get over the notion that you were a certain alien."

"A certain—" Diller started strangling. He stopped breathing entirely for a moment, then resumed slowly, through distended nostrils. "I remember," he said. "I saw this *thing* coming across the field, with a bunch of people trailing after it, and I wondered what it was. Then something went wrong in my head. I didn't wait any more. I just ran like hell and got behind a building. Something going on in my head kept bugging me, and I wanted to get closer to it but I knew that was wrong, and I wondered if I was going crazy, and then, aarrrghgh—" Diller stopped and swallowed; his eyes were mad with fear until he could breathe again.

"All right, Diller, it's all right," Skarwold kept repeating. Diller's breathing went back to normal, but he didn't talk. Skarwold said, "I'd like to introduce Mr. Garner of the United Nations Technological Police."

Diller gave a polite nod. His curiosity was plain. Garner

said, "We'd like to catch this alien before he does any more damage. If you don't mind, I think you may have some information that we don't."

Diller nodded.

"About five minutes after that telepathic blast hit you, the alien took off for outer space. An hour later he was followed by a man who has reason to believe that *he* is the alien. He has false memories. They're both headed in the same general direction. They're after something. Can you tell me what it is?"

"No," said Diller.

"You may have gotten something in that mental blast. Please try to remember, Diller."

"I don't remember anything, Garner."

"But—"

"You old fool! Do you think I want to choke to death? Every time I start to think about what happened I start strangling! I start thinking funny too; everything looks strange. I feel surrounded by enemies. But worst of all, I get so *depressed*! No. I don't remember anything. Get out."

Garner sighed and ostentatiously put his hands on the chair controls. "If you change your mind—"

"I won't. So there's no need to come back."

"I won't be able to. I'm going after them."

"In a spaceship? You?"

"I've got to," said Garner. Nevertheless he glanced involuntarily at his crossed legs—crossed this morning, by hand. "I've got to," he repeated. "There's no telling what they want, but it must be something worthwhile. They're going to too much trouble to get it. It could be a weapon, or a signal device to call their planet."

The travel chair whirred.

"Half a minute," said Diller.

Garner turned off the motor and waited. Diller leaned back and looked up at the ceiling. His face began to change. It was no longer an expression he wore, a mirror

80

of his personality, but a random dispersal of muscle tension. His breathing was ragged.

Finally he looked up. He started to speak and failed. He cleared his throat and tried again. "An amplifier. The —the bastard has an amplifier buried on the eighth planet."

"Fine! What does it amplify?"

Diller started to choke.

"Never mind," said Garner. "I think I know." His chair left the room, going much too fast.

"They're both runnin' scared," said Luke. "Headed for Neptune at one gee, with your husband an hour and a half behind."

"But aren't you sending someone after him?" Judy begged. "He isn't responsible, he doesn't know what he's doing!"

"Sure. We're sending me. He's got my partner, you know." Seeing Mrs. Greenberg's reaction, he quickly added, "They're in one ship. We can't protect Lloyd without protecting your husband."

They sat in Judy's hotel room sipping Tom Collinses. It was eleven hundred of a blazing August morning.

"Do you know how he got away?" Judy asked.

"Yah. The ET knocked everybody crosseyed when he threw that tantrum at the port. Everybody but Greenberg. Your husband simply picked out a ship that was on standby and had Lloyd take it up. Lloyd knows how to fly a Navy ship, worse luck."

"Why would Mr. Masney be taking Larry's orders?"

"Because Larry hypnotized him. I remember the whole performance."

Judy looked down at her lap. The corners of her mouth began to twitch. She began to giggle, and then to laugh. Just as the laughter threatened to become sobs, she clenched her teeth hard, held the pose for a moment, then sagged back in her chair.

"I'm all right now," she said. Her face held no laughter, only exhaustion.

"What was that all about?"

"It doesn't matter. Why would they be going to Neptune?"

"I don't know. We're not even sure that's where they're going. Don't you have some sort of telepathic link with your husband?"

"Not any more. Since he went into Dr. Jansky's time field I can't feel anything any more."

"Well, it wouldn't feel like him anyway. Do you remember how you felt at twenty hours night before last?"

"At twenty? Let me see." She closed her eyes. "Wasn't I asleep . . . ? Oh. Something woke me up and I couldn't go back to sleep. I had the feeling that something was terribly wrong. Monsters in the shadows. I was right, wasn't I?"

"Yes. Especially if it was Larry's mind you felt." He gave that a moment to sink in. "And since then?"

"Nothing." Her small hand tapped rhythmically on the chair arm. "Nothing! Except that I want to find him. Find him! That's all I've wanted since he took the ship! Find him before he . . ."

Find it! But there was no question of finding it, he told himself for the hundredth time. He had to find it first! He had to find it before Kzanol, the real Kzanol, did. And for the hundredth time he wondered if he could.

The Earth had been invisible for hours. Kzanol/Greenberg and Masney sat speechless in the control bubble, speechless and motionless. The control bubble was three quarters of the ship's living space. One could stand upright only in the airlock.

There weren't many distractions for Kzanol/Greenberg.

True, he had to keep an eye on Masney. He had to do more than that. He had to know when Masney was uncomfortable, and he had to know it before Masney knew it. If Masney ever came out of hypnosis it might be difficult to get him back. So Kzanol/Greenberg had to send Masney to the lavatory; had to give him water before he was thirsty; had to exercise him before his muscles could cramp from sitting. Masney was not like the usual slave, who could take care of himself when not needed.

Other than that, the self-styled ptavv was dead weight.

He spent hours at a time just sitting and thinking. Not planning, for there was nothing to plan. He either reached the eighth planet first, or he didn't. Either he put on the amplifier helmet, or the real Kzanol did, and then there would be no more planning, ever. No mind shield could face an amplifier helmet. On the other hand, the helmet would make him Kzanol's master. Using an amplifier on a thrint was illegal, but he was hardly in danger of thrintun law.

(Would an amplifier boost the Power of a slave brain? He pushed the thought aside—again.)

The far future was bleak at best. He was the last thrint; he couldn't even breed the real Kzanol to get more. Yes, he would be master of an asteroid belt and a heavily populated slave world; yes, he would be richer than even Grandfather Racarliw. But Grandfather had had hundreds of wives, a thousand children!

Kzanol/Greenberg's hundreds of wives would be human slaves, as would his thousand children. Lower-than-ptavvs, every one.

Would he find "women" beautiful? Could he mate with them? Probably. He would have to try it; but his glands were emphatically not Kzanol's glands. In any case he would choose his women by Larry Greenberg's standards of beauty—yes, Greenberg's, regardless of how he felt, for

83

much of the glory in being rich is showing it off, and he would have nobody to impress but slaves.

A dismal prospect.

He would have liked to lose himself in memories, but something held him back. One barrier was that he knew he would nevermore see Thrintun the homeworld, nor Kzathit where he was born, nor Racarliwun, the world he had found and named. He would never look at the world through his own eye; he would see himself only from outside, if ever. This was his own body, his fleshly tomb, now and forever.

There was another barrier, a seemingly trivial matter. Several times Kzanol/Greenberg had closed his eyes and deliberately tried to visualize the happy past; and always what came to mind were whitefoods.

He believed Garner, believed him implicitly. Those films could not have been faked. Copying an ancient tnuctip inscription would not have been enough to perpetrate such a fraud. Garner would have had to *compose* in tnuctip!

Then the bandersnatchi were intelligent; and the bandersnatchi were undeniably whitefoods. Whitefoods were intelligent, and always had been.

It was as if some basic belief had been shattered. The whitefoods were in all his memories. Whitefoods drifting like sixty-ton white clouds over the estates of Kzathit Stage Logs, and over the green-and-silver fields of other estates when little Kzanol was taken visiting. Whitefood meat in a dozen different forms, on the family table and in every restaurant waiter's memorized menu. A whitefood skeleton over every landowner's guest gate, a great archway of clean polished white bone. Why, the thrint hadn't been born who didn't dream of his own whitefood herd! The whitefood gate meant "landowner" as surely as the sunflower border.

Kzanol/Greenberg cocked his head; his lips pursed slightly, and the skin puckered between his eyebrows. Judy would have recognized the gesture. He had suddenly realized what made the intelligent whitefood so terrible.

A thrint was master over every intelligent beast. This was the Powergiver's primal decree, made before he made the stars. So said all of the twelve thrintun religions, though they fought insanely over other matters. But if the whitefood was intelligent, then it was immune to the Power. The tnuctipun had done what the Powergiver had forbade!

If the tnuctipun were stronger than the Powergiver, and the thrintun were stronger than the tnuctipun, and the Powergiver were stronger than the thrintun—

Then all priests were charlatans, and the Powergiver was a folk myth.

A sentient whitefood was blasphemy.

It was also very damned peculiar.

Why would the tnuctipun have made an intelligent food animal? The phrase had an innocuous sound, like "overkill" or "euthanasia," but if you thought about it—

Thrintun were not a squeamish race. Power, no! But—

An intelligent food animal! Hitler would have fled, retching.

The tnuctipun had never been squeamish, either. The lovely simplicity of their mutated racing virprin was typical of the way they worked. Already the natural animal had been the fastest alive; there was little the tnuctipun could do in the way of redesigning. They had narrowed the animal's head and brought the nose to a point, leaving the nostril like a single jet nacelle, and they had made the skin almost microscopically smooth against wind resistance, but this had not satisfied them. So they had removed several pounds of excess weight and replaced it with extra muscle and extra lung tissue. The weight removed had been all of the digestive organs. A mutated racing viprin had a streamlined sucker of a mouth which opened directly into the bloodstream to admit predigested pap.

The tnuctipun were always efficient, but never cruel.

Why make the whitefood intelligent? To increase the

size of the brain, as ordered? But why make it immune to the Power?

And he had eaten whitefood meat.

Kzanol/Greenberg shook his head hard. Masney needed attention, and he had planning to do. Didn't he? Planning, or mere worrying?

Would the amplifier work on a human brain?

Could he find the suit in time?

" 'Find him,' " Garner quoted. "That could fit. He's looking for something he believes he needs badly."

"But you already knew that. It doesn't help."

"Mrs. Greenberg, what I really came for is to find out everything you can tell me about your husband."

"Then you'd better talk to Dale Snyder. He got here this morning. Want his number?"

"Thanks, I've got it. He called me too. You know him well?"

"Very."

"I'll also want a chance to talk to Charley, the dolphin anthropologist. But let's start with you."

Judy looked unhappy. "I don't know where to start."

"Anywhere."

"Okay. He's got three testicles."

"I'll be damned. That's fairly rare, isn't it?"

"And sometimes troublesome, medically, but Larry never had any problems. We used to call it 'that little extra something about him.' Is this the kind of thing you're after?"

"Sure." Luke didn't know. He remembered that the better he knew the man he was chasing, the more likely he was to catch him. It had worked when he was a cop, decades ago. It ought to work now. He let her talk, interrupting very rarely.

"I never noticed what a practical joker he was until after he began working with dolphins, but he's told me some of the things he pulled at college. He must have been a real terror. He was terrible at team athletics, but he plays fair squash and demon tennis . . ." She needed no prompting now. Her life came out in a stream of words. Her life with Larry Greenberg.

" . . . must have known a lot of women before he met me. And vice versa, I might add. Neither of us has ever tried adultery. I mean, we have an arrangement that we *can*, but we've never used it."

"You're sure?"

"Absolutely." Luke saw that she was. She was amused that he should have to ask.

". . . It shocks him when I can make a prediction that accurate. I don't think he really believes in prescience, so it scares him when I get a flash. He thinks it's some sort of magic. I remember one day, we'd been married less than a year, and I'd gone out on a shopping spree. He saw me come in with a load of packages, and when I dumped them and went out and came back with the second load he said, 'Honest to God, beautiful, you're spending blue chips like the Last War was starting tomorrow!' I didn't say anything. I just gave him this brave little smile. He went absolutely white. . . ."

Relevant or irrelevant, it was all coming out. Judy talked faster and faster. She was doing just what he'd told her to, but with an urgency that was puzzling.

". . . Most of the couples we know never got married until someone was pregnant. When you pass the Fertility Board you hate to risk throwing it away by marrying a sterile partner, right? It's too big a thing. But we decided to take the chance." Judy rubbed her throat. She went on hoarsely. "Besides, the 'doc had okayed us both for parenthood. Then there was Jinx. We had to be sure neither of us got left behind."

"By me that was good thinking. Mrs. Greenberg, I'll quit now, while you've still got a voice. Thanks for the help."

"I hope it did help."

The speed at which she'd talked—the detail. Luke sent the elevator straight to the top. He knew now why she'd painted so complete a portrait of Larry Greenberg. Whether she knew it or not, she didn't expect to see him again. She'd been trying to make him immortal in her memory.

❦

The Jayhawk Hotel was the third tallest building in Topeka, and the rooftop bar had a magnificent view. As he left the elevator Luke met the usual continuous roar. He waited ten seconds while his ears "learned" to ignore it: an essential defense mechanism, learned by most children before they were three. The hostess was a tall redhead, nude but for double-spike shoes, her hair piled into a swirling, swooping confection which brought her height to an even eight feet. She led him to a tiny table against a window.

The occupant rose to meet him. "Mr. Garner."

"Nice of you to do this for me, Dr. Snyder."

"Call me Dale."

Garner saw a dumpy man with an inch-wide strip of curly blond hair down the center of his scalp. Temporary skin substitute covered his forehead, cheeks and chin, leaving an X of unharmed skin across his eyes, nose, and the corners of his mouth. His hands were also bandaged.

"Then I'm Luke. What's your latest word on the Sea Statue?"

"When the Arms woke me up yesterday afternoon to tell me Larry had turned alien. How is he?"

Avoiding details, Luke filled the psychologist in on the past twenty-four hours. "So now I'm doing what I can on the ground while they get me a ship that will beat Greenberg and the ET to Neptune."

"Brother, that's a mess. I never saw the statue, and if

I had I'd never have noticed that button. What are you drinking?"

"I'd better grab a milk shake; I haven't had lunch. Dale, why did you want us to bring the statue here?"

"I thought it would help if Larry saw it. There was a case once, long before I was born, where two patients who both thought they were Mary, Mother of God, showed up at the same institution. So the doctors put them both in the same room."

"Wow. What happened?"

"There was a godawful argument. Finally one of the women gave up and decided she must be Mary's mother. She was the one they eventually cured."

"You thought Greenberg would decide he was Greenberg if you showed him he wasn't the Sea Statue."

"Right. I gather it didn't work. You say they can use my help at Menninger's?"

"Probably, but I need it first. I told you what I think Greenberg and the Sea Statue are after. I've got to chase them down before they get to it."

"How can I help?"

"Tell me everything you can about Larry Greenberg. The man on his way to Neptune has an extraterrestrial's memories, but his reflexes are Greenberg's. He proved that by driving a car. I want to know what I can count on from the Greenberg side of him."

"Very little, I'd say. Count on something from the Greenberg side of him and you'd likely wind up naked on the Moon. But I see your point. Let's suppose the, uh, Sea Statue civilization had a law against picking pockets. Most countries had such laws, you know, before we got so crowded the cops couldn't enforce them."

"I remember."

Snyder's eyes widened. "You do? Yes, I suppose you do. Well, suppose Larry in his present state found someone picking his pocket. His impulse would be to stop him, but not to yell for a policeman. He'd have to make a conscious decision to do that. This would be unlikely until after the fight was over and he'd had time to think."

"If I caught him by surprise I could count on his human reflexes."

"Yes, but don't confuse reflexes with motivations. You don't know what his motivations are now."

"Go on."

Snyder leaned back and folded his hands behind his head. A waiter glided up and produced drinks from a well in its torso. Garner paid it and shooed it away.

Abruptly Snyder was talking. "You know what he looks like: five feet seven inches tall, dark and fairly handsome. His parents were Orthodox, but they weren't millionaires, they couldn't afford a fully kosher diet. He's very well adjusted, and he has enormous resilience, which is why he was able to take up contact telepathy.

"He does have some feelings about his height, but nothing we need bother about. They are partly compensated by what he calls 'that little extra something about me.'"

"Mrs. Greenberg told me."

"Partly he means his telepathy. Partly it's the medical anomaly I assume Judy mentioned. But he's in dead earnest in regarding himself as something special.

"You might also remember that he's been reading minds for years, human and dolphin minds. This gives him an accumulation of useful data. I doubt if the dolphins are important, but there were physics professors, math students, and psychologists among the volunteers who let Larry read their minds by contact. You could call him superbly educated." Snyder straightened. "Remember this, when you go out after him. You don't know the Sea Statue's intelligence, but Larry has his own intelligence and nobody else's. He's clever, and adaptable, and unusually sure of himself. He's suspicious of superstition but genuinely religious. His reflexes are excellent. I know. I've played tennis with him: Judy and I against him alone, with Larry guarding the singles court."

"Then I'd better stay alert."

90

"Absolutely."

"Suppose his religion was threatened. How would he react?"

"You mean Orthodox Judàism?"

"No, I mean any religion he now happens to hold. Wait, I'll expand that. How would he react to a threat against something he's believed in all his life?"

"It would make him angry, of course. But he's not a fanatic. Challenge him and he'd be willing to argue. But to make him change his mind about something basic, you'd have to offer real proof. You couldn't just cast doubts. If you see what I mean."

On the great white screen in the Space Traffic Control Center, two dark blobs hung almost motionless. Halley Johnson swung his phone camera around so Garner could see it.

"The military ship is going just a teeny bit faster than the honeymooner. If they're really going all the way to Neptune they'll pass each other."

"Where else could they be going?"

"A number of asteroids. I have a list."

"Let's hear it."

Johnson read off the names of fourteen minor Greek deities. "A lot more have been crossed off," he added. "When the ship passes turnover point and keeps accelerating, we mark it out."

"Okay. Keep me posted. How 'bout my ship?"

"Be here at twenty. You'll be in orbit by twenty-one."

The Struldbrugs' Club is not the only club with a lower age limit on its members. (Consider the Senate.) It is the only club whose age limit rises one year for every two that passes. In 2106 every member was at least one hundred and forty-nine years old. Naturally the Struldbrugs' autodocs were the best in the world.

But the treatment tanks still looked like oversized coffins.

Luke pulled himself out of the tank and read the itemized bill. It was a long one. The 'doc had hooked by induction into his spine and done deep knee bends to build up muscle tone; recharged the tiny battery in his heart; and added hormones and more esoteric substances to his bloodstream. Localized ultrasonic pulses had applied the Ch'ien treatment; Luke could feel the ache from the base of his skull all the way down his spine, to where sensation almost disappeared in the small of his back. A manicure and pedicure had finished the checkup.

Luke used his Arm ident to punch for a six months' supply of the hormones, antiallergens, selective pest killers, and general rejuvenators which kept him alive and healthy. What came out of the slot was a hypodermic the size of a beer can, with instructions all down the sides in fine print. Luke tightened his lips at the sight of the needle; but you can't use a spray hypo when you've got to hit the vein. He told the 'doc where to send the bill.

One more chore and he could take a cat nap.

Because of the decrepit state of many Struldbrugs, the club phone booths had been made large enough for travel chairs—barely. Already Luke had the air translucent with cigarette smoke. "How do you talk to a dolphin?" he asked, feeling unaccountably diffident.

Fred Torrance said, "Just the way you would have talked to Larry. But Charley will answer in dolphinese, and I'll translate. You couldn't make out his English over the phone."

"Okay. Charley, my name's Lucas Garner. I'm with the Arms. Do you know what's happened to Larry?"

Grunts, chortles, whistles, squeals, and squeaks! Only once had Luke heard the like of it. Eighteen years ago he had been a witness at a murder trial. Three other witnesses—and the victim, who of course was not present —had been dolphins.

Torrance translated: "He knows Larry's lost his sense of identity. Dr. Jansky called and told us all about it."

"Well, yesterday Larry got away from us and took off in a stolen ship. I'm going after him. I want to know everything Charley can tell us about him."

Dolphin language. Torrance said, "Charley wants a favor in return."

"Oh, really? What?" Luke braced himself. Since the cracking of the swimmer-dolphin language barrier, the dolphins had proved very able bargainers. Fortunately or not, the dolphins' rigid, complex moral code had adapted easily to the walker concept of trade.

"He wants to talk to you about the possibility of dolphins taking part in the seeding of the stars."

Of the three present, Torrance the seadoc had the clearest understanding of what was being said. Charley was speaking slowly and clearly, staying well below the ultrasonic range, but even so Torrance often had trouble translating. To him the bilingual conversation went like this:

"I'll be damned in writing," said Garner. "Charley, is this a new idea? I've never heard of a dolphin wanting to go starhopping."

"Not . . . brand new. The question has been discussed on the abstract level, and many are in favor of it, if only from the fear that swimmers will be left out of something. But I, myself, never felt the urge until three days ago."

"Greenberg. He had the space bug bad, did he?"

"Please use the present tense. Yes, he has the bug all right. I've had a couple of days to get used to Larry in my head. I won't say I quite understand this urge to reach Jinx, but I can explain a little of it.

"I dislike using an outmoded term, but part of it is"—Charley used the English words— " 'anifesst desstinee. Part is the fact that on Jinx he could have as many children as he wants, four or five even, and nobody would complain. Partly it is the same urge I sometimes get in this tank. No room to swim. Larrry wants to walk down a street without the slightest fear of stepping on someone's toes, having his pocket picked, or getting

93

caught in a pedestrian traffic jam and being carried six blocks the wrong way. Notice that I've put considerably more thought into analyzing this than Larrry ever did."

"And how do you feel about it? You're a dolphin. You probably never looked at the stars—"

"Missterr 'Arrnerr, I assure you that we swimmers know what the stars look like. There are many astronomy and astrophysics tapes in the illustrated texts your agents sold us. And, after all, we do have to come up for air sometimes!"

"Sorry. But the point remains: you've got plenty of elbow room, you've never had your toes stepped on, and nothing but a killer whale could possibly be interested in picking your pocket. So what's in it for you?"

"Perhaps adventure. Perhaps the forming of a new civilization. You know that there has been only one swimmer civilization for many thousands of years. The seas are not isolated, as are the continents. If there is a better way of doing things, the way for us to find out is to build many communities on many worlds. Is this logical?"

"Yes!" There was no mistaking the emphasis in Garner's voice. "But it may not be as easy as you think. We'd certainly have to design you an entirely new ship, because we'd have to include swimming water. And water is heavy, dammit. I'll bet shipping a dolphin would cost ten times as much as shipping a man."

"You use water for reaction mass for the landing motors. Could you put lights in the water tanks?"

"Yes, and we could fill them only two-thirds full, and we could install filters to remove the fish and the algae and so on before the water reaches the motors. We could even install small tanks somewhere that you could ride in while the tanks were being emptied during landing. Charley, are you beginning to get some picture of the cost of all this?"

"Beginning to, yes. Money is complex."

"You know it. But you couldn't possibly buy your way on, not with what the dolphins produce. Oh, you could get a pair to Wonderland, but how could two dolphins stay sane alone? What would they live on? Seeding an ocean isn't like planting a wheat field, even when you have to make the topsoil yourself. Fish swim away! Seeding an ocean has to be done all at once!

"Hmm. You can't even claim it's your right to be on a starship. Dolphins don't pay UN taxes . . . hmm," said Luke, and scratched his scalp. "Charley, just how many dolphins could be persuaded to leave their oceans forever?"

"As many as we need. Selected by lot, if necessary. The Law permits such selection in cases of extreme need. Of the hundreds of swimmers who took part in early walker experiments to prove us intelligent, and of the twenty or thirty who died as a result, nearly all had been so selected."

"Oh . . . really? And nobody ever guessed." Torrance wondered at Garner's peculiar expression. Almost a look of horror. It had been so long ago; why should he be so shocked? Garner said, "Let it pass. How many genuine volunteers?"

"They would all be genuine. But you want to know how many would volunteer without the lots? No more than fifty to a hundred, I would think, out of all the oceans."

"All right. Now what we'll have to start with is a massive advertising campaign. The dolphins will have to contribute a share of the cost of a dolphin spaceship. Just a gesture. It would be nominal compared to the final cost, but to you it will be expensive. Then we'll have to convince most of the walker world that a planet without dolphins isn't worth living on. Needless to say, I already believe this."

"Thank you. Thank you for all of us. Would swimmers be taking part in this advertising?"

"Not directly. We'd want pronouncements, statements from prominent swimmers like the one the newspapers call the Lawyer. You know who I mean?"

"Yes."

"Understand that I'm just guessing. We'll have to hire a 'public opinions consultant,' a publicity agent, and let him do the work. And it might be all for nothing."

"Could we lower the cost by shipping swimmers in Doctor Jansskee's time retarder field?"

Garner looked utterly astonished. Torrance grinned, recognizing the reaction: Is This A Dolphin Talking? "Yes," said Garner, nodding to himself. "Right. We won't even need tanks. Let the humans do the crew work, and keep you frozen until they can find and seed a small sea, like the Mediterranean . . ."

It went on and on.

". . . So it's settled," said Garner, a long time later. "Talk it over with the dolphins, especially the ones with power, but don't make a move until I get back. I want to pick a publicity agent. The right publicity agent."

"I hate to remind you, but isn't there a chance you won't come back?"

"Holy Hannah! I completely forgot." Garner glanced down at his wrist. "There goes my cat nap. Quick, Charley, start talking about Greenberg. What's your opinion of him?"

"Prejudiced, I'm afraid. I like him and envy him his hands. He is very alien to me. And yet, perhaps not." Charley let himself sink to the bottom of the tank. Torrance took the opportunity to clear his throat, which felt like he'd been eating used razor blades.

Charley surfaced and blew steam. "He is not alien. Negative! He thinks a lot like me, because he took contact from me several times before we chanced it the other way around. He is a practical joker—no, that is very far from the true concept. Well, it will have to do. Larrry is a dolphin type of practical joker. Years ago he selected a few of our most famous jokes, old japes which we consider classics, translated them into something he could use as a walker, and then decided not to use them because he might go to prison for it. If he is no longer afraid of prison he might be tempted to play his jokes."

"Uh huh."

"Such as something I have not tried yet with a swimmer. I must use the English word: hypnotism."

Torrance said, "I didn't get that."

"Defined as an induced state of monomania."

"Oh, *hypnotism.*"

"Larrry has studied it thoroughly, and even tried it out, and for him it works. On a swimmer it might be ineffective."

"He's already tried it," said Garner. "Anything else?"

"Garrnnrr, you must understand that the dolphin gurgle-buzz-SQUEEEE is *not* truly a practical joke. It is a way of looking at things. Putting a monkey wrench in machinery is often the only way to force somebody to repair, replace, or redesign the machinery. Especially legal or social machinery. Biting off somebody's fin at exactly the right time can change his whole attitude toward life, often for the better. Larrry understands this."

"I wish I did. Thanks for your time, Charley."

"Negative! Negative! Thank you for yours!"

An hour to the long jump. Luke's throat felt well used. He might still have time for a fifteen-minute cat nap, but he'd wake up feeling worse than ever.

He sat in the Struldbrugs' reading room and thought about Greenberg.

Why had he become an alien? Well, that was easy. With two sets of memories to choose from, he'd naturally chosen the identity most used to sorting itself out from other identities. But why cling to it? He must know by now that he was not the Sea Statue. And he'd had a happy life as Larry Greenberg.

His wife was something to envy—and she loved him. According to Dr. Snyder, he was stable, well adjusted. He liked his work. He thought of himself as something special.

But the Sea Statue was all alone in the universe, the last of its race, marooned among hostiles. The Greenberg

Sea Statue had also lost his ability of—well, telepathic hypnosis was close enough.

Any sane person would rather be Greenberg.

Garner thought, I'll have to assume that Greenberg as Greenberg literally cannot think with the Sea Statue memories in his mind. He must remain the Sea Statue to function at all. Otherwise he'd have at least *tried* to change back.

But—that peculiar arrogance he'd displayed under interrogation. *Not a—slave. Not human.*

A robot bonged softly next to his ear. Garner turned and read in flowing light on the waiter's chest: "You are requested to call Mr. Charles Watson at once."

Chick Watson was fat, with thick lips and a shapeless putty nose. He wore crew-cut, bristly black hair and, at the moment, a gray seventeen-hundred shadow over cheeks and jaw. He had a harmless look. Centered on his desk was a large screen viewer running film at abnormal speed. Not one in a thousand could read that fast.

A buzzer sounded. Chick snapped off the reader and turned on the phone. For a fat man he moved quickly and accurately.

"Here."

"Lucas Garner calling, sir. Do you want to see him?"

"Desperately." Chick Watson's voice belied his appearance. It was a voice of command, a deep, ringing bass.

Luke looked tired. "You wanted me, Chick?"

"Yeah, Garner. I thought you could help me with some questions."

"Fine, but I'm pressed for time."

"I'll make it quick. First, this message from Ceres to Titan Enterprises. The *Golden Circle* made a takeoff under radio silence yesterday, from Topeka Base, and the Belt intends to submit a bill for tracking. Titan sent the notice here. They say their ship must have been stolen."

"That's right. Kansas City has the details. It's a very complicated story."

"An hour later the Navy ship *Iwo Jima*—"

"Also stolen."

"Any connection with the Sea Statue incident at UCLA?"

"Every connection. Look, Chick—"

"I know, get it from Kansas City. Finally . . ." Chick fumbled among the spools of film on his desk. His voice was suspiciously mild as he said, "Here it is. Your notification that you'll be leaving Topeka on a commandeered Navy ship, the *Heinlein*; departure: Topeka Base at twenty-one hundred; destination: unknown, probably Neptune; purpose: official business. Garner, I always said it would happen, but I never really believed it."

"I haven't gone senile, Chick. This is urgent."

"Fastest attack of senility I ever heard of. What could possibly be urgent enough to get you into space at your age?"

"It's that urgent."

"You can't explain?"

"No time."

"Suppose I order you not to go."

"I think that would cost lives. Lots of lives. It could also end human civilization."

"Melodramatic."

"It's the literal truth."

"Garner, you're asking me to assume my own ignorance and let you go ahead on your own because you're the only expert on the situation. Right?"

Hesitation. "I guess that's right."

"Fine. I hate making my own decisions. That's why they put me behind a desk. But, Garner, you must know things

99

Kansas City doesn't. Why don't you call me after take-off? I'll be studying in the meantime."

"In case I kick off? Good idea."

"Don't let it slip your mind, now."

"Sure not."

"And take your vitamins."

Like a feathered arrow the *Golden Circle* fell away from the sun. The comparison was hackneyed but accurate, for the giant triangular wing was right at the rear of the ship, with the slender shaft of the fusilage projecting deep into the forward apex. The small forward wings had folded into the sides shortly after takeoff. The big fin was a maze of piping. Live steam, heated by the drive, circled through a generator and through the cooling pipes before returning to start the journey again. Most of the power was fed into the fusion shield of the drive tube. The rest fed the life-support system.

In one respect the "arrow" simile was inexact. The arrow flew sideways, riding the sun-hot torch which burned in its belly.

Kzanol roared his displeasure. The cards had failed again! He swept the neat little array between his clublike hands, tapped them into deck formation, and ripped the deck across. Then, carefully, he got to his feet. The drive developed one terran gravity, and he hadn't quite had time to get used to the extra weight. He sat down at the casino table and dug into the locker underneath. He came out with a new deck, opened it, let the automatic shuffler play with it for a while, then took it out and began to lay it out solitaire style. The floor around him was littered with little pieces of magnetized plastic card.

Perhaps he could think up some fitting punishment for the pilot, who had taught him this game.

The pilot and copilot sat motionless in the control room. From time to time the pilot used his hands to change course a trifle. Every fourteen hours or so the co-pilot would bring Kzanol a bowl of water and then return to her seat. Actinic gas streamed from the belly of the ship, pushing it to ever higher velocities.

It was a beautiful night. Years had passed since Garner last saw the stars; in the cities they couldn't shine through the smog and the neon glare, and even the American continents were mostly city. Soon he would see them more clearly than he had in half a century. The air was like the breath of Satan. Garner was damp with sweat, and so were Anderson and Neumuth.

"I still say we could do this by ourselves," said Anderson.

"You wouldn't know what to look for," Garner countered. "I've trained myself for this. I've been reading science fiction for decades. Centuries! Neumuth, where are you going?"

Neumuth, the short dark one, had turned and was walking away. "Time to get strapped down," he called back. "Bon voyage!"

"He's going forward, to the cockpit of the booster," said Anderson. "We go up that escalator to the ship itself."

"Oh. I wish I could see it better. It's just one big shadow."

The shadow was a humped shadow, like a paper dart with a big lizard clinging to its back. The paper glider was a ramjet-rocketplane, hydrogen fueled in the ramjet and using the cold liquid hydrogen to make its own liquid oxygen in flight. The slim cylinder clinging to its upper surface was a fusion drive cruiser with some attachments for rescue work. It carried two men.

Using its fusion motor in Earth's atmosphere would have been a capital offense. In taking off from ground eighteen hours earlier, Masney and Kzanol/Greenberg had broken twelve separate local laws, five supranational regulations and a treaty with the Belt.

Another ship roared a god's anger as it took off. Garner blinked at the light. "That was our rendezvous ship," Anderson said matter-of-factly.

Luke was tired of having to ask silly-seeming questions. He wasn't going to like Anderson, he decided. If the kid wanted to tell him why they needed a rendezvous ship, he would.

They had reached the bottom of the escalator. "Meet you at the top," said Garner, reaching into his ashtray. Anderson stared, jolted, as an invalid's travel chair became a flying saucer. An Arm using an illegal flying machine? An *Arm*?

Anderson rode up the stairs, whistling. This trip might be fun after all.

"Just leave the chair on the escalator platform," he said at the top. "We've made arrangements to have it delivered to the local Struldbrugs' Club. They'll take good care of it. I'll carry you in, sir."

"You get my medikit. I'll walk," said Garner. And he did, wobbling and using his arms freely. He barely reached his gee chair. Anderson found the medikit and followed. He checked Garner's crash web before he used his own.

"Neumuth? Ready," said Anderson, as if into empty air. He continued, "The other ramjet-rocket carried a bundle of solid fuel rockets as big as this ship. They're strap-ons. We don't have any more power than the *Golden Circle,* and we're a day and a half behind them, so we use the strap-ons to give us an initial boost. Inefficient, but if it works—"

"—It's good," Garner finished for him. His voice was thickened by the pull of the linear accelerator. For five seconds the soundless pressure lasted, two gravities of pull. Then the rams fired and they were off.

It would take two days of uncomfortable two-gee acceleration to get there first, thought Garner, compressed in his chair. His old bones would take a beating. Already he was missing the gadgets in his own chair. This trip wasn't going to be fun.

Lars was eating a very messy sardine-and-egg sandwich when the buzzer buzzed. He put it down gently, using both hands, so that it wouldn't bounce in the nearly nonexistent gravity. He wiped his hands on his coverall, which he washed frequently, and went to the transceiver.

The maser beam had crossed the void in one instantaneous beep. The radio translated it into sound, then thoughtfully scaled it down against the minute Doppler shift. What came out was the colorless voice of Cutter, duty man at Ceres.

"Thank you, Eros, your message received in full. No more emergencies this time, Lars. Topeka Base called us eight hours ago, giving us the time of takeoff and predicted course. According to your report the takeoff was four minutes late, but that's typical. Keep us posted.

"Thank you, Eros, your—"

Lars switched it off and went back to his sandwich. Briefly he wondered if Cutter had noticed that the Navy ship was following the two he had tracked eighteen hours ago. No doubt he had.

"You're taking it too hard," said Dale Snyder.

Judy shrugged.

Again Dale took in the puffy eyelids showing beneath the makeup, the unfamiliar lines in Judy's pretty twenty-eight-year-old face, the death-grip on her coffee glass, her rigid position in what should have been an easy chair. "Look here," he said. "You've got far too many things working on you. Have you considered—I mean, have you given any thought to invoking your agreement with Larry concerning adultery? At least you could eliminate *one* of your tensions. And you're not helping him by worrying."

"I know. I've thought about it. But—" she smiled, "not with a friend, Dale."

"Oh, I didn't mean that," Dale Snyder said hastily. And blushed. Fortunately the bandages covered most of it. "What about going to Vegas? The town's full of divorcees of both sexes, most of them temporarily terrified of getting married again. Great for a short-term affair. You could cut it short when Larry comes back."

He may have put too much assurance into the last sentence, because Judy's grip tightened on her glass and relaxed immediately. "I don't think so," she said listlessly.

"Think about it some more. You could even do some gambling."

Two gravities! Twelve hours ago he would have sneered at himself. Two gravities, lying on his back? Luke could have done it on his head. But that was twelve hours ago, twelve hours of double weight and throbbing metal and noise and no sleep. The strap-on fission/fusion motors roared in pairs outside the hull. Two had been dropped already. Ten remained, burning two at a time. It would be a day and a half before ship's weight returned to normal.

The stars were hard, emphatic points. Never had the sky been so black; never had the stars been so bright. Luke felt that they would have burned tiny holes in his retinae if he could have held his eyes fixed on one point. Tiny multicolored blindnesses to add to his enviable collection of scars. The Milky Way was a foggy river of light, with sharp actinic laser points glaring through.

So here he was.

He'd been seventy-two the day they launched the first passenger ship: an orbital craft, clumsy and spavined and oversized by today's standards, nothing more than a skip-glider. They'd told him he was too old to buy a ticket. What was he now? He wanted to laugh, but there was pressure on his chest.

With an effort he turned his head. Anderson was locking a sheet of transparent plastic over part of the complex wraparound control panel. Most of the panel was already under the plastic sheets. He saw Luke looking at him, and he said, "Nothing to do from now on but watch for rocks. I've put us above the plane of the Belt."

"Can we afford the extra time?"

"Sure. If they're going to Neptune." Anderson's voice came cheerful and energetic, though slurred by the extra weight on his cheeks. "Otherwise they'll beat us anyway, to wherever they're going. And we won't know it until they make turnover."

"We'll have to risk that."

The extra weight wasn't bothering Anderson at all.

One gravity is standard for manned spacecraft. Some rescue ships, and a few expresses in the Belt, have attachments for clusters of fusion/fission strap-on engines to cut their transit time. Often it makes sense. More often it doesn't. Given continuous acceleration, the decrease in trip time varies as the square root of the increase in power. Greenberg and the ET should have expected their pursuers, had they known of them, to stay a day and a half behind all the way to Neptune.

A strap-on can only be used once. The smooth cylindrical shell contains only hydrogen gas under pressure and a core of uranium alloy. The fusion shield generator is external; it stays with the ship when the strap-on falls away. The moment the shield forms on the inside of the shell, neutrons from the core begin to reflect back into the uranium mass, and everything dissolves in the chain reaction. As time decreases the pressure inside the trapped star, the tiny exhaust aperture is designed to wear away, keeping the acceleration constant.

This time the strap-ons were vital. The *Heinlein* would beat the others to Neptune by six hours—

If they were headed for Neptune! But if Diller were wrong, or if Diller had lied—if Diller, like Greenberg, thought he was an alien—if the fleeing ships were en route to some asteroid—then the *Heinlein* would overshoot. When the others made turnover it would be too late. The *Heinlein* would be going too fast.

Of course, there were always the missiles. And the Belt would consider it a violation of treaty if the *Golden Cir-*

cle or the *Iwo Jima* landed in the Belt. They might be persuaded to attack.

But there was Lloyd Masney.

With a full minute's delay in transmission, his discussion with Chick Watson had been both tiring and unproductive. Now Chick knew everything he knew, except for the exhaustive details he'd collected on Greenberg's life. They'd reached some obvious decisions. They would not send any more ships from Earth, ships which would obviously arrive far too late to help. Earth would fire at sight if either of the target ships reached anywhere and started back. Chick would keep his communications open for Garner, ready to search out any information he might need. And one other decision—

"No, we can't call on the Belt for help." Chick's expression dismissed the idea with the contempt he felt it deserved. "Not with Belt relations the way they are now. They know what they'd do to us with an embargo on uranium, and we know what we'd do to them by holding off their vitamins, and both sides are just itching to see who'd collapse first. You think they'd believe a story like ours? All the proof we can offer is second hand, from their point of view. They'd think we were setting up our own mining operation, or trying to claim a moon. They'd think anything at all, because all they can tell for sure is that three ships from Earth are on their way to Neptune.

"Worse yet, they might just assume that this telepathy amplifier won't reach beyond Earth. In which case they could make a better deal with Greenberg, king of the world, than they can with us."

"I'll never buy that," Garner had answered. "But you're right, there's no point in crying for help. There may be a better answer."

And so they waited. If they were right, if the stolen ships were going to the eighth planet, they would be turning in six days. Luke and Anderson had nothing to do until the ET's gave them their orders.

Luke went to sleep, finally, smiling. He smiled because the gees were pulling on his cheeks. Anderson was sleeping too, letting the autopilot do the work.

At twenty-one hundred the next day the last pair of strap-ons burned out and were dropped. Now six tumbling pairs of thick-walled metal cylinders followed the *Heinlein* in a line millions of miles long. In a century all would reach interstellar space. Some would eventually pass between the galaxies.

The ship went on at a comfortable one gee. Luke scowled ferociously to exercise his facial muscles, and Anderson stepped into the airlock to do isometric exercises.

The rocks of the Belt slipped by below, faster every second.

He was a clerkish-looking man with a droning voice, and he called himself Ceres Base. From his appearance he might never have had a name of his own. He wanted to know what an Earth Navy ship was doing in the Belt.

"We have passage," Anderson told him curtly.

Yes, said Ceres, but what is the *Heinlein*'s purpose? Garner whispered, "Let me have the mike."

"Just talk. He can hear you."

"Ceres, this is Lucas Garner, Arm of the UN. Why the sudden shift?"

"Mr. Garner, your authority does not exist here in—"

"That's not what I asked."

"I beg your pardon?"

"You just now realized we're following the *Golden Circle*. Didn't you?"

"Are you really? To what purpose?"

"None of your business. But I may tell one of your superiors, if you pick the right superior. Get him on fast, were getting further away every minute."

"The Belt will not allow you passage unless you explain your purpose here."

"The Belt won't touch us. Good-by."

At the sound of the bell Marda rolled off the couch and walked smoothly into the phone booth. Already there was only a slight pull in her abdomen from the surgical cement, though the operation was just twelve hours old. A slight pull when she moved, to remind her of what she had lost.

"Lit!" she called. "Ceres. It's for you."

Lit trotted in from the garden.

Cutter looked apprehensive for once. "Remember the two bandit ships from Topeka Base? Someone's joined the procession."

"Took them long enough. We warned them days ago. When did it take off?"

"Two days ago."

"*Two days,* Cutter?"

"Lit, the *Heinlein* gave us plenty of warning and an accurate course projection. She also used strap-on boosters. The time/position curve looks completely different from the curves for the bandits. It took me this long to see that everybody's going in the same direction."

"Damn it, Cutter—never mind. Anything else?"

"The *Heinlein*'s passing Ceres now. Do you want to talk to Lucas Garner, Arm of the UN?"

"An Arm? No. What's an Arm doing out here?"

"He won't say. He might tell you."

"What makes you so sure the Belt won't stop us?"

"Well, they can't catch us and board us. All they could do is throw missiles at us, right?"

"You make me so happy."

"Belters aren't stupid, Anderson. Uh, oh."

A space-tanned Caucasian with black hair and wrinkled eyes looked out of the screen at them and said, "Do I have the honor of addressing Lucas Garner aboard the *Heinlein*?"

"Right. Who's this?"

"Charles Martin Shaeffer. First Speaker, Belt Political section. May I ask—"

" 'Little' Shaeffer?"

The mahogany man's face froze for an instant, then barely smiled. "They call me Lit. What are you up to, Garner?"

"You I'll tell, Shaeffer. Now don't interrupt, because it's a long story. . . ."

It took fifteen minutes to tell. Shaeffer listened without comment. Then there were questions. Shaeffer wanted details, clarification. Then some of the questions were repeated. There were veiled accusations, which became less veiled. Anderson kept the beam fixed and sensibly let Luke do the talking. After an hour of question-and-answer, Luke shut it off.

"That's as much cross examination as I'm taking today, Shaeffer."

"What did you expect me to do, swallow your tale whole? Your opinion of Belters needs revision."

"No, Shaeffer, it doesn't. I never expected to be believed. You can't afford to believe me; the propaganda value would be enormous if Earth took you in on such a wild story."

"Naturally. On the other hand, what you're trying to tell me is that an alien monster is threatening all of human civilization. In view of this it seems odd that you object to answering a few questions."

"Nuts. Shaeffer, do this. Send a few armed—"

"I'm *not* taking orders—"

"Don't interrupt me, Shaeffer. Send a few armed ships to follow me to Neptune. I'm sure that's where they're going; they've already passed turnover for most of the asteroids. It'll take your ships a while to catch us. They may get there in time to help us out, and they may not. If you think I'm a liar, then send your ships along only to make sure I don't do any poaching. Regardless of what you suspect me of, you'll need ships to stop me, right? But arm them, Shaeffer. Arm them good.

"Your only other choice is to start a war, right? Right. If you want my story confirmed call the Arms office in Los Angeles, then call the UN Comparative Cultures Exhibit in Brasilia Ciudad and ask if they've still got the Sea Statue. That's all you can do. So call me back and tell me how many ships you're sending." Luke gestured to Anderson, who turned him off.

"Jerk," said Anderson, with feeling.

"Not at all. He did the right thing. He'll keep on doing it. First he'll send ships after us, including one with antiradar which will have to get there later than the others because of the extra weight. He'll call Earth and get my story confirmed as well as he can. The worst he can think of me then is that I'm thorough. Finally he'll call us and tell us he's sending one less ship than he is, leaving out the antiradar. That ship gives the Belt every chance to catch me red-handed, doing whatever illegal treaty-breaking thing they think I'm doing, especially since I don't know the Belt's discovered antiradar—"

"Uh huh."

"But if they don't catch me at anything then they cooperate with me."

"Uh huh. It's perfect. But will they be able to handle it when we turn out to be telling the truth?"

"Sure. They'll be armed for us, and a weapon is a weapon. Besides which, some of them will believe me. Belters, they're always waiting for the first alien contact. They'll be armed for bear, regardless." Garner rubbed his scalp. "I wonder what the Sea Statue is armed for?"

A dry tooth socket is not extremely painful. The pain is mild. What drives the unfortunate victim to thoughts of suicide is, the pain never lets up. There is no escape.

Marda felt the gentle, reminding pull in her abdomen every time she moved.

Many Belt women were childless. Some had been spayed by solar storms. Some were frigid, and their frigidity let them endure the loneliness of a singleship. Some had undesirable recessive genes; and, contrary to popular terran belief, the Belt had fertility laws. Some could not conceive in free or nearly free fall. They were a special class, the exiles from Confinement.

What was Lit doing in that phone booth? It had been over an hour.

He was furious, she could see that. She'd never seen him so mad. Even after the screen went dark, he just sat there glaring at the screen.

Something made Marda get up and push open the soundproof door. Lit looked around. "That Arm. That flatlander. Marda, can you imagine an Arm getting huffy with *me*?"

"He really pushed all your buttons, didn't he? What happened, Lit?"

"Oh . . ." Lit banged the heels of his hands together. "You remember those two ships that took off from To-peka Base without—"

"I never heard about it."

"Right. I forgot." She'd hardly been in a mood to listen then. "Well, two days ago . . ."

By the time he finished he was almost calm. Marda felt safe in saying, "But, Lit, you cross-examined him for a full hour. What else could he do but cut you off or admit he was lying?"

"Good point. What I'm really mad about is that tale he told me."

"You're sure he was lying? It sounds almost too fantastic."

"Aw, honey. It *is* too fantastic."

"Then forget it."

"That's not the point. What's he want with Neptune? Why's he need three ships? And why, in the name of Reason, does he commandeer the *Golden Circle* from Titan Enterprises?"

"To back up his story?"

"No. I think it's the other way around. His story was tailored to fit the facts."

Slowly he turned back to face the blank screen. He sat for a while, with Marda watching him, and then he said, "I'm going to have to do just as he told me. That burns me. Remind me to tell you someday why I hate Arms."

"Okay. Later today, then."

"Good girl." But he'd already forgotten her. Still he stared at the blank screen, not willing to give Ceres its orders until he'd thought them out completely. Finally he muttered, "I can get the jump on him. I'll send the ships from the lead Trojans; he'll be passing right over them. We'll be after him faster than he thinks." His hand darted out. "And—mph. I can send a radar proof. Operator? Get me a maser to Achilles, fast."

Of course, the whole ploy could be a red herring, he thought, waiting for the operator to call back. A distraction for something going on right here in the Belt. Well, they won't get away with that either. Every ship that leaves Earth or the Moon is going to be questioned. We'll board some of them, and follow the ones that won't allow it. Earth will get its share too. I'll make our espionage system think the end of the world is coming.

Four and a half days later neither Kzanol nor Kzanol/ Greenberg had turned ship. It seemed they really were going to Neptune. If so they would be turning in eighteen hours.

It was already time for Anderson to turn ship. He did. "We'll get there six hours ahead of them," he told Garner.

"Good."

"Of course, they could be headed for outer space. It could be a coincidence that they're going in that direction. Then we'll lose them."

"In those ships? Besides, I never doubted they were going to Neptune. I just didn't want to take chances."

"Uh huh. I'm just hypothesizing. How about some lunch?"

"Good." It was high noon. The life-support system didn't include enough room to walk around in, but it did have a mechanized kitchen; and one thing the space conquerors had learned early was that caviar is cheaper than corn flakes. Caviar has far more food value per payload ounce. So Garner and Anderson ate prefrozen crepes Veronique and wondered how long it would be before they could exercise off the extra pounds.

While they were feeding the plates back into the food slot, Garner found something else to worry about. "Can we turn our telescope around?"

"Sure. Why?"

"To follow the other ships. They're still ahead of us, and we're moving ass-backwards."

"We can't see them now because the glare of our exhaust blocks our view. But we'll be passing them in six hours, and we can watch them from then on."

"We'll never catch them," said the man in the lead ship. He was a tall, spindly Negro with prematurely white hair and an habitual poker face. "They'll be three days ahead of us all the way. Poachers!"

Somebody, Smoky from his accent, said, "It'd be four if we hadn't started from Achilles."

"Something on the scope," said one of the other ships. All five were singleships, hurriedly converted to war potential from their mining duties in the lead cluster of Jupiter's Trojan asteroids.

"Like what?"

"Specks of hydrogen light. Moving almost as fast as the Arm, judging by the red shift. Way ahead of him."

"Is it too late to call Ceres?"

"Direct, yes. She'll be behind the Trojans for a while."

"Tartov! Call Phoebe and say that there are three ships past Uranus, all en route to Neptune, all moving at approx the same speed. I want ETAs for each of them."

"I hear you, Lew."

The fleet of five ships looked like a small swarm of fireflies. They were only thousands of miles apart; they stayed that close to avoid irritating message delays. The distance would still have hidden them from each other if they had been using chemical fuels or ion jets, but the searing light of the fusion drives showed brighter than any of the surrounding stars.

"Lew?"

"Here."

"I'm sure one of them is a honeymoon special. It's got a strong oxygen line in its spectrum."

"Yeah? The Arms are thorough, you've got to give them credit."

Tartov said, "They must be after something big. Something tremendous."

None of the others spoke. Perhaps they were reserving judgment. Behind the swarm, falling further behind with each second, a lone firefly struggled in pursuit.

Something went by like a falling comet, if there were such a thing. "There goes Greenberg," said Anderson, grinning. The blue-white light faded slowly into the background of stars.

"The *Golden Circle* should be by in a few minutes," he added. "Greenberg's ship is just a touch faster."

Garner didn't answer.

Anderson turned to look at him. "Something bugging you?" he asked kindly.

Garner nodded. "I've been thinking about it for days. I just now realized that there isn't any good answer. It's like trying to keep a teleport in jail."

"What is?"

"Trying to keep either of those birds from picking up the amplifier."

He slapped his chair absently for the cigarette button, caught himself and scowled. "Look. We can't get to it first. We don't know how they plan to find it themselves. Probably they just remember where they put it. We don't even know how big it is! We can't arrest them; at least we can't arrest the ET because he'd just turn us into spare butlers, and we'll have trouble with Greenberg because he's got an armed ship and Masney can use the guns. He may be better than you, son." Garner looked horribly like a Greek tragic mask, but his voice was the voice of a very worried man. "It seems to me that the only thing we can do is shoot on sight."

"You can't do that!" Anderson protested. "You'll kill Greenberg and Masney both!"

"I don't want to kill anyone. Give me another choice!"

"Well, give me a chance to! I haven't even thought about it yet!" He screwed his young face into a smooth semblance of Garner's. "Hey!" he exclaimed suddenly. "Yeah, I've got something. You don't have to shoot on sight. You can wait to find out if what they're looking for is really on Neptune."

"What good will that do?"

"They could have left something on one of the moons, or in orbit. But if it's on Neptune, they can't get at it! Neither of their ships develops more than one gee. Neptune's pull is higher than that. They can't land."

"No good. The ET has a winged ship. But that's good thinking anyway, son."

"You bet it is," Anderson said angrily. "How the hell is he going to get back up?"

Luke Garner looked like he'd seen a vision. After a moment he asked, "Son, have you ever thought of joining the Arms?"

"Why—" Anderson began modestly.

Who are you?

The two stared at one another.

WHO ARE YOU???????

"Lucas Launcelot Garner. Arm."

"Leroy. George Anderson's boy. The astronaut."

I DON'T WANT YOU FOLLOWING ME. The Mind was blasting, angry. Even when merely "thinking aloud," it held Garner and Anderson physically and mentally paralyzed. Then it came to a decision. Anderson reached toward the control panel. His fingernails rapped against plastic. He began fumbling at the catches on the guard panel.

Garner pushed him back with one hand.

It lashed him. Garner felt it stop his heart, and he gasped, horribly. Right now? he wondered. His sight turned red and went out.

He came back to life with a singing in his head. Anderson was looking terribly haggard. He had a spray hypo in his hand. "Thank God," he blurted. "I thought you were gone."

"Heart stopped," Garner wheezed. (Not this time.) "First time it's ever happened. What did you use?"

"Adrenalin in the heart. Are you all right?"

"Sure. Considering."

The young pilot was still pale. "You know what he told me to do? I was going to turn off the fusion shield! They'd have seen it on Earth." He shuddered. "In daylight they'd have seen it! Very lucky thing you stopped me. But how did you know?"

"I knew what he wanted for a result. Never mind. How did you know it was my heart?"

"I felt him do it. Well, we don't have to worry about him until we get to Neptune. He went out of range right after he stopped your heart."

"We'll have to shoot first with that bird."

"It'll be a pleasure," Anderson said furiously.

Kzanol strained to hang onto the enemy minds, but it was no use. Not only was distance against him; the difference in velocities was even more of a barrier. A slight relativistic difference in time rates could make communication impossible, even between two thrints.

He turned his attention back to the cards. The pilot, who was English, called this game Patience. It was well named. Kzanol was learning patience the hard way. The floor of the lounge was littered with scraps of torn plastic; but this one deck had already survived ten lost games. It was the last deck on board.

Growling deep in his throat, like the carnivore he was, Kzanol scraped the cards together and shuffled them. He was learning coordination, too. And he had learned something about himself: he would not let a slave see him cheating at cards. He had cheated once, and the pilot had somehow guessed. He would not cheat again.

Kzanol jumped. Another one! This one was too far to the side to control, but easily close enough to sense. And yet . . . the image had a fuzziness that had nothing to do with distance. As if the slave were asleep. But . . . different.

For half an hour it stayed within reach. In that time Kzanol satisfied himself that there was no other slave on board. He did not think of another thrint. He would have recognized the taste of a thrint command.

At six hundred hours the next morning, Greenberg's ship turned around. Three minutes later the *Golden Circle* did the same. Anderson found the prints in the scope camera when he woke up: two lights which stretched slowly into bright lines, then contracted with equal deliberation into somewhat brighter points.

The time passed slowly. Garner and Anderson were already deep in a tournament which they played on the viewer screen: a rectangular array of dots to be connected by lines, with victory going to the player who completed the most squares. Almost every day they raised the stakes.

On the morning of the last day Garner got back to even. At one point he had been almost eleven thousand dollars in debt. "See?" he said. "You don't give up all your pleasures as you get older."

"Just one," Anderson said thoughtlessly.

"More than that," Garner admitted. "My taste buds have been wearing out for, lo, these many years. But I guess someday someone will find a way to replace them. Just like my spinal cord. That wore out too."

"Wore out? You mean—it wasn't an accident? The nerves just—died?"

"Just went into a coma would be more like it."

A swift change of subject was in order. "Have you got any better idea of what we do when we get to Neptune? Do we hide on one of the moons and watch?"

"Right," said Garner.

But half an hour later he asked, "Can we reach Earth from here?"

"Only by maser," Anderson said dubiously. "Everyone on Earth will be able to listen in. The beam will spread that far. Have you got any secrets from the man on the slidewalk?"

"Don't worry about it. Aim a maser at Earth."

It took half an hour for Anderson to center the beam and set it tracking. "If it's 'Love to Mother,' you're dead," he warned Garner.

"My mother passed away some time ago. In fact, it's been just about a century. And she thought she was an old woman! Hello, Arm Headquarters. This is Lucas Garner calling the United Nations Technological Police."

Anderson nudged him with an elbow. "Are you waiting for an answer, shnook?"

"Of course not!" Habits are hard to break. "This is Garner calling Arm Headquarters, Earth. Please aim your reply at Neptune. We urgently need the following information from Dorcas Jansky. Does his retarder field stop radar completely? Repeat, completely. Would the ET suit do the same?" He put down the mike. "Okay, son, repeat that a few times."

"All right, it's on repeat. Now what was that all about?"

"I don't know why it took me so long to figure it out," Garner said smugly. "The ET has been frozen for about two billion years, according to Greenberg. I think he was telling the truth. He couldn't know that there's something on Neptune unless he put it there two billion years ago. And how could he assume that it hasn't fallen apart or rusted to death or whatever, after all that time?"

"It's in a retarder field."

"Right."

Anderson looked at the chron. "You'll be getting your answer in a little over eight hours, not counting the time it takes to get what's-his-name. Figure an hour; they'll be calling around nineteen thirty. So let's get some sleep. We'll be coming in about three tomorrow morning."

"Okay. Sleeping pills?"

"Uh huh." Anderson punched buttons on the medicine box. "Luke, I still think you were waiting for Earth to answer."

"You can't prove it, son."

Twenty-one forty-five. Garner studied the board for a

moment, then drew one short line between two dots of light. The scanner, set to follow the movements of the tip of his stylus, reproduced the line on the board.

The radio boomed to life.

"This is Arm Headquarters calling spaceship *Heinlein*. Arm Headquarters calling Lucas Garner, spaceship *Heinlein*. Garner, this is Chick. I got hold of Jansky this morning, and he spent three hours doing experiments in our lab. He says a retarder field does, repeat does, reflect one hundred percent of energy of any frequency, including radar, and including everything he could think of. Visible, ultraviolet, infrared, radio, X rays. If you're interested, he thinks there's a mathematical relation between a retarder field and a fusion shield. If he finds one, do you want to know? Is there anything else we can help you with?"

"You can help me with this game," Luke muttered. But Anderson had erased it, along with the six-inch curve Luke had drawn when he jerked his arm at the sound of the radio.

The man in the lead ship ran fingers through his cottony hair like a man sorely puzzled. He barely had room in the tiny control bubble. "All ships," he said. "What the hell did he mean by that?"

After a few moments someone suggested, "Code message." Others chorused agreement. Then Tartov asked, "Lew, does Earth have something called a retarder field?"

"I don't know. And there's nowhere we can beam a maser that some Earth ship won't get in it." He sighed, for masers are always a chore to use. "Someone ask the Political Section about retarder fields."

"Retarder fields?"

"Retarder fields. And they sent us the full text of the message to Garner."

Lit smiled with one side of his mouth. "Retarder fields

120

were part of Garner's story. I knew he'd be thorough, but this is ridiculous." He thought of the thousands of Belt ships he'd put on standby alert, just in case Garner's fleet was intended to distract attention from things closer to home; and he thought of five mining ships and a priceless radar proof headed for what might as well be outer space. Garner was causing more than his fair share of activity. "All right, I'll play his silly game. Beam Arm Headquarters and ask them what they know about retarder fields."

Cutter was shocked. "Ask the Arms?" Then he got the joke, and his face was chilled by a smile. On Cutter a smile always looked false.

It wasn't until Arm Headquarters cautiously denied all knowledge of retarder fields, that Lit Shaeffer began to have doubts.

With the first jarring clang of the alarm Garner was awake. He saw Anderson groan and open his eyes, but the eyes weren't seeing anything. "Meteor strike!" he bawled.

Anderson's eyes became aware. "Not funny," he said.

"No?"

"No. Are you the type who yells 'Red Alert' on a crowded slidewalk? What time is it?"

"Oh three oh four." Garner looked out at the stars. "No Neptune. Why?"

"Just a sec." Anderson fooled with the attitude jets. The ship swung around. Neptune was a blue-green ball, dim in the faint sunlight. Usually a world that close is awe-inspiring, if not blinding. This world only looked terribly cold. "There it is. What'll I do with it?"

"Put us in a search orbit and start scanning with the radar. Can you set it to search for something as dense as dwarf star matter?"

"You mean, set it to search below the crust? Will do, Captain."

"Anderson?"

"Uh huh?" He was already at work on the instrument panel.

"You will remember that we have a time limit?"

Anderson grinned at him. "I can put this thing in a forced orbit and finish the search in five hours. Okay?"

"Great." Luke started punching for breakfast.

"There's just one thing. We'll be in free fall some of the time. Can you take it?"

"Sure."

Anderson moved in. When he finished, the ship balanced nose down, one thousand miles above the surface, driving straight at the planet with a force of more or less one gee. The "more or less" came from Anderson's constant readjustments.

"Now don't worry," Anderson told him. "I'm trying to keep us out of the atmosphere, but if we do happen to land in the soup all I have to do is turn off the motor. The motor is all that's holding us in this tight orbit. We'd fall straight up into outer space."

"So that's what a forced orbit is. How are you working the search?"

"Well, on a map it would look like I'm following the lines of longitude. I'll turn the ship sideways for a few minutes every time we cross a pole, so we can keep changing our line of search. We can't just let the planet turn under us. It would take almost sixteen hours."

The world rolled beneath them, one thousand miles below—more or less. There was faint banding of the atmosphere, but the predominant color was bluish white. Anderson kept the radar sweeping at and below the forward horizon, which on the radar screen looked like thin, stratified air. It was solid rock.

"Understand, this is just to find out if it's *there*," Anderson said an hour later. "If we see a blob, we'll have it pinned within five hundred miles. That's all."

"That's all we need."

At nine hours Anderson turned the ship around, facing outward. He ached from shoulders to fingertips. "It's not there," he said wearily. "Now what?"

"Now we get ready for a fight. Get us headed toward Nereid and turn off the drive."

The bright stars that were two fusion-drive spacecraft were too close to the tiny Sun to be easily seen. Anderson couldn't even find the *Golden Circle*. But Greenberg's ship came steadily on, blue and brightening at the edge of the Sun's golden corona. Garner and Anderson were on a ten-hour path to Nereid, Neptune's outermost moon. They watched as Greenberg's light grew brighter.

At nine thirty the light began to wiggle. Greenberg was maneuvering. "Do we start shooting?" Anderson wanted to know.

"I think not. Let's see where he's going."

They were on the night side of the planet. Greenberg was diving toward Neptune at a point near the twilight line. He was clearly visible.

"He's not coming toward Nereid," said Anderson. They were both whispering, for some reason.

"Right. Either he left it on Triton, or it's in orbit. Could it be in orbit after that long?"

"Missile's tracking," Anderson whispered.

Greenberg was past Triton before he started to decelerate. "In orbit?" wondered Garner. "He must have been nuts."

Twenty minutes later Greenberg's ship was a wiggling light between the horns of Neptune's cold blue crescent. They watched its slow crawl toward one of the horns. He was in a forced orbit, covering a search pattern of the surface. "Now what?" Anderson asked.

"We wait and see. I give up, Anderson. I can't understand it."

"I swear it's not on Neptune."

"Uh, oh." Garner pointed. "Hail, hail, the gang's all here." A tiny spear of light was going by the lighted edge of the planet.

The blue-green ball was larger than he had anticipated. For the first time Kzanol regretted his carelessness in not finding out more about the eighth planet when he had the chance, some two billion years ago. He asked the pilot and copilot, who remembered that Neptune had 1.23 gee at surface. Earth gee, of course. For Kzanol it would be about two and a half.

Kzanol stood at one of the small windows, his jaw just above the lower edge, his leathery lips drawn back in a snarl of worry. Not long now! One way or another. For the pilot was nudging the ship into a search orbit.

Someone was already there.

It was the half-asleep free slave he'd passed at the halfway point. He was almost around the curve of the world, but he would be back in eighteen diltun or so. Kzanol had the pilot put the *Golden Circle* in orbit and turn off the motor. Let the slave do the searching.

The ship went by underneath, spitting fire at the stars. The slave was indeed marking out a search pattern. Kzanol let him go on.

And he wondered. How was he going to get down, on a motor which simply didn't have the power?

He let the pilot think about it, and the pilot told him. On rockets, wings, and rams, all going at once. But even the pilot couldn't think of a way back up.

Kzanol/Greenberg, of course, had no warning at all. At its present setting his radar would have shown Kzanol's ship as more transparent than air. Even the planet itself was translucent. Kzanol/Greenberg kept watch over the radar screen, sure that if Masney missed the suit, he wouldn't.

"Why isn't the other ship searching too?" Anderson wondered. "It's just floating."

"Ordinarily," said Garner, thinking out loud, "I'd think they were in cahoots. There's no need for them both to search. But how—? Oh. I get it. The ET has taken control of Masney and Greenberg. Either that or he's letting them do his job for him without their knowing it."

"Wouldn't the job get done quicker if they both searched?"

"I'm beginning to wonder if this alien isn't the aristocrat's aristocrat. Maybe he thinks that anyone who works is a slave. Since he's a master . . . But the real question is, what are they searching for, and where is it?

"Look, son, why don't you warm up the radio and point the maser at our fleet of Belters. I might as well fill them in."

One thing about the Belt ships: at least the air plant could handle pipe tobacco. The man in the third ship was the only man in the fleet who took advantage of the fact, one of exactly six in the entire Belt. He was known, not too affectionately, as Old Smoky.

Once he had been a flatlander. For nearly thirty years he had piloted a succession of circumlunar tourist boats. His nights he had spent in a small, cheap apartment a few stories above the vehicular traffic level in Los Angeles. On holidays he went to the beach, and was lucky to find enough clear sand to sit on; his vacations were spent in foreign cities, strange and novel and undeniably fascinating but generally just as crowded as Los Angeles. Once he stayed two weeks in what was left of the Amazon jungle. He smuggled some cigarettes in with him, risking two years in prison, and ran out in five days. When he found he was telling every friend and stranger how much he wanted a smoke, he went back to the cities.

He had met Lucas Garner in the line of duty; Garner's duty. There was a massive sit-in to protest rumored corruption in the Fertility Board; and when the law hauled Smoky off the top strip he met Garner in the uniform of a police chief. Somehow they got to be friends. Their respective views on life were just close enough to make for violent, telling, fun arguments. For years they met

125

irregularly to argue politics. Then Luke joined the Arms. Smoky never forgave him.

One day Smoky was rounding the Moon nose down with a load of tourists, when he felt a sudden, compelling urge to turn nose out and keep driving until all the stars were behind him. He fought it down, and landed in Death Valley that evening as he had landed seven-thousand-odd times before. That night, as he approached his apartment through the usual swirling mob, Smoky realized that he hated every city in the world.

He had saved enough to buy his own mining ship. Under the circumstances the Belt was glad to have him. He learned caution before the Belt killed him, and he earned enough to keep his ship in repair and himself in food and tobacco.

Now he was the only man in the fleet who could recognize Lucas Garner's voice. When the radio burst to life he listened carefully to the message, then called Lew to report that it really was Garner.

For Smoky, the broadcast removed all doubt. It was Garner himself. The old man was not above a judicious lie, but he was not prone to risk his life. If he was near Neptune in a leaky terran Navy crate, he must have an outstanding reason to be there.

Thoughtfully Old Smoky checked through his arsenal of two radar missiles, one heat seeker, and a short-range laser "cannon." The war of the worlds was here at last!

∽≈∾

Kzanol was baffled. After six hours of searching, the slave Masney had covered the entire planet. The suit wasn't there!

He let the slave begin his second search, for the sake

126

of thoroughness. He took his own ship to Triton. The Brain could not compute the course of moons; one of them may have gotten in the way of the ship as it speared toward Neptune. Very likely it had been Triton. That moon was not only closer than Nereid, it was far bigger: 2500 miles thick as compared to 200.

A nerve-wracking hour later, an hour of flying upside down over Triton's surface with the jet firing outward and the lightly pitted moon showing flat overhead, Kzanol admitted defeat. No white flash had shown itself on the radar screen, though Neptune itself had glowed through the transparent image of the larger moon. He turned his attention to the small moon.

"So that's it!" Anderson's face glowed. "They thought it was on the surface and it wasn't. Now they don't know *where* it is!" He frowned in thought. "Shouldn't we get out of here? The honeymooner's aiming itself at Nereid, and we're too close for comfort."

"Right," said Garner. "But first we turn the missile loose. The one that's homed on the alien. We can worry about Greenberg later."

"I hate to do it. There're two other people on the *Golden Circle*." A moment passed. Lengthened. "I can't move," said Anderson. "It's that third button under the blue light."

But Luke couldn't move either.

"Who'd have thought he could reach this far?" he wondered bitterly. Anderson couldn't help but agree. The ship continued to fall toward Nereid.

To the Power, distance was of little importance. What mattered was numbers.

Nereid was a bust. The deep radar went through it as through a warped window pane, and showed nothing. Kzanol gave it up and watched the half-asleep slave for a while. His tiny flame burned bravely against the Neptunian night.

Kzanol was in a bad state of mind. It seemed that his

ship had missed not only Neptune but both its moons. What could have gone wrong with the Brain? Probably it had never been intended to last three hundred years. But deep in the bottom of his mind, he knew better. The Brain had missed deliberately. Kzanol had ordered it to commit suicide, not realizing what he asked. The Brain —which was a machine, not a slave, not subject to the Power—had disobeyed. His ship must have hurtled through the solar system and gone on into interstellar space at .97 light. By now it would be beyond the curve of the universe.

He felt the muscles pulling at his mouth, flattening the eating tendrils against his cheeks to protect them, opening his jaws as wide as they would go, and wider, pulling his lips back from the teeth until they were ready to split. It was an involuntary reaction, a reaction of fear and rage, automatically readying the thrint for a battle to the death. But there was nothing to fight. Soon Kzanol's jaws closed and his head drooped between his massive shoulders.

All in all, the only pleasure he had was to watch the last ship searching Neptune for the third time—and to see its bright flame suddenly lengthen, then shorten again. The sleepy slave had given up.

Then Kzanol knew that he too was going to Triton. A feeling of noble pity stole over him, and he remembered the tradition that the family of Racarliw had never mistreated a slave. Kzanol went to meet the sleeper at Triton.

"One . . . two . . . I can't find Garner's ship. He must have landed somewhere, or turned off his drive. The others are just milling around."

"Funny he hasn't called us. I hope nothing's happened to him."

"We'd have seen the explosion, Smoky. Anyway, he was going for Nereid when his drive stopped. If it failed, we can find him later."

When Kzanol was close enough, he Told the sleeper to turn ship and join him. In an hour the Navy ship and the *Golden Circle* were alongside.

Kzanol's pilot and copilot were worried about the fuel situation, so as soon as the sleeper's ship was close enough Kzanol Told him to transfer his fuel to the *Golden Circle*. He waited while various clanking and banging sounds rang through the ships. Fortunately the cards were magnetized, and there was webbing to hold him in his seat. He followed the movements of his three personal slaves with the back of his mind: the sleeper near the tail, the pilot and copilot motionless in the cockpit. He didn't want to risk their lives by letting them help the sleeper.

Naturally he jumped like a terrified gazelle when his airlock door swung open and a slave walked in.

A slave with a mind shield.

"Hi!" it said, incomprehensibly in English. "I guess we'll need a translator." And it coolly walked forward to the control room. At the door it stopped and gestured—with Kzanol's disintegrator.

A man of Leeman's talent and education should never have been given such a boring job. Leeman knew it could never have happened in the Belt. Someday soon he would migrate to the Belt, where he would be appreciated.

Meanwhile, Geoffrey Leeman was the foreman of the Lazy Eight III's skeleton maintenance crew.

Leeman envied the crew of the other section, the drive section at Hamburg. Busybodies with good intentions were constantly ordering minor changes in the starship's drive while they waited for politics to let them launch. The Lazy Eight III's life system hadn't been altered in two years.

Until today.

Now Leeman and his three subordinates watched a horde of technicians doing strange things to the number three "stateroom." A complete balloon of fine wire mesh was being strung over the walls, floor, and ceiling. Heavy machinery was being welded to what would be the ship's floor and was now the outer wall. Taps were let into the power system. Leeman and his men found themselves running errands through the ring-shaped corridor, bringing coffee and sandwiches and detail diagrams, tools and testing machinery and cigarettes. They had no idea what was going on. The newcomers were willing to answer questions, but the answers were gibberish. As:

"We'll be able to *triple* the number of passengers!" said the man with a head like a speckled brown egg. He shook an ammeter for emphasis. "Triple!"

How?

The man waved his ammeter to include the room. "We'll have them standing in here like rush-hour commuters in an elevator," he confided. When Leeman accused him of levity he became mortally offended and refused to say another word.

By the end of the day Leeman felt like a flatworm in a four-dimensional maze.

Somehow he managed it so that the entire group went to dinner together, for mutual brain-picking. Things became clearer during dinner. Leeman's ears went up when he heard the phrase "retarder field."

Dinner turned into a party. It was almost two hundred before Leeman could make a phone call. The other man almost hung up. But Leeman knew the words to stop him.

The Lings' first honeymoon had been spent at Reno, Nevada, thirty years ago. Since then Ling Wu had become rich in wholesale pharmaceuticals. Recently the Fertility Board had granted the couple the rare privilege of having more than two children. And here they were.

Here, before the crystal wall of the main dance bubble, looking out and down at a ringed and banded world. They didn't hear the music behind them. It was magic music, the sound of imagination, brought to life by the

130

wild, desert loveliness before them. Soft curves of ice ran out to a horizon like the lip of a nearby cliff; and above the cliff hung a bauble, a decoration, an aesthetic wonder such as no habitable world has ever known.

Ask an amateur astronomer about Saturn. He won't just tell you; he'll drag out his telescope and show you. He'll break your arm to show you.

Ling Dorothy, fourth generation San Franciscan, pushed the palms of her hands against the crystal wall as if half wanting them to go through. "Oh, I hope, I hope," she said, "I hope it never comes for us!"

"What, Dot?" Ling Wu smiled up at her, for she was an inch taller than he was.

"The *Golden Circle*."

"It's five days late already. I love it here too, but I'd hate to think people died just to let us stay a little longer."

"Haven't you heard, Wu? Mrs. Willing was just telling me that somebody stole the *Golden Circle* right off the spaceport field!"

"Mrs. Willing is a romantic."

"Givvv me ti', givvv me ti'," Charley mimicked. "First Larrry, then 'Arrnerr. Time is all we get. Do they want the stars all for themselves?"

"I think you underrate them," said the older dolphin.

"Surely there's room for both of us on any world." Charley hadn't been listening. "They practically didn't know we were *here* until a short time ago. We could be useful, I know we could."

"Why shouldn't they have time? Do you know how much time they themselves needed?"

"What do you mean?"

"The first walker story about a trip to the moon is thousands of years old. They didn't get there until a hundred and fifty years ago. Have a little patience," said the one with the worn teeth and the scarred jaw.

"I don't have thousands of years. Must I spend my life looking at the sky until my eyes dry out?"

"You wouldn't be the first. Not even the first swimmer."

Dale Snyder walked down the hall like a conqueror planning new conquests. When he passed patients he smiled and nodded, but his brisk walk discouraged conversation. He reached the door to the nurses' lounge and turned in.

It took him fifteen seconds to reach the coffee stand. In that time Dale Snyder aged forty years. His body sagged; his shoulders slumped; his cheeks slid half an inch downward, leaving a mask of puffy-eyed discouragement. He poured a foam-plastic cup of black coffee, regarded it with curled lip, and poured it down the drain. A moment of indecision before he refilled the cup from another spiggot. Yerba mate. At least it would taste different.

It did. He flowed into a chair and stared out the window, the cup warming his hand. Outside, there were trees and grass and what looked like brick walks. Menninger's was a labyrinth of buildings, none more than four stories tall. A mile-high skyscraper would have saved millions in land, even surrounded by the vitally necessary landscaping; but many woman patients would have run screaming from the sexual problems represented by such a single, reaching tower.

Dale shook himself and gulped at the brew. For ten minutes he could forget the patients.

The patients. The "alien shock" patients. They had fooled him at first, him and others, with their similar behavior. Only now was it becoming obvious that their problems were as different as their fingerprints. Each had gone into some kind of shock when the alien cut loose. Dale and his colleagues had tried to treat them as a group. But that was utterly wrong.

Each had borrowed exactly what he needed from the

132

ET's tantrum of rage and shock and grief and fear. Each had found what he had needed or feared. Loneliness, castration syndrome, fear of violation, xenophobia, claustrophobia—there was no point even in cataloguing the list.

There weren't enough doctors. There wasn't room for the number of doctors they would need. Dale was exhausted—and so was everyone else. And they couldn't show it.

The cup was empty.

"On your feet, soldier," Dale said aloud. At the door he stood aside for Harriet Something, a cheerfully overweight woman who looked like everybody's mother. His mind held the afterimage of her smile, and he wondered, how does she do it? He didn't see the smile drain away behind his back.

"It's the details," said Lit. "The double damned details. How *could* they have covered so many details?"

"I think he told you the truth," Marda said decisively.

Lit looked at his wife in surprise. Marda was notoriously slow to reach decisions. "Don't get me wrong," he said. "The Arms *could* have attended to all these—little things. What bothers me is the work it must have taken. Hiding Greenberg. Coaching his wife. Tearing things up in the starship's life system. They can put everything back later, of course, but imagine going to all that trouble! And the disturbance at Menninger's. My God, how *could* they have worked that? Training all those patients! And they flatly couldn't have borrowed the *Golden Circle*. Ninety millionaires at the Titan Hotel are all screaming murder because they can't go home on time. Thirty more on Earth are going to miss their honeymoon trips. Titan would never have let that happen! The Arms must have out-and-out *stolen* that ship."

"Occam's Razor," said Marda.

"Occam's—? Oh. No. Either way, I have to make just too many assumptions."

"Lit, how can you take the chance? If Garner isn't lying, the whole solar system's in danger. If he is, what's his motive?"

"You're really convinced, aren't you?"

Marda bobbed her head vigorously.

"Well, you're right. We can't take the chance."

When he came out of the phone booth he said, "I just sent the fleet the record of my interview with Garner. The whole bloody hour. I'd like to do more, but Garner'll hear everything I say. At this distance he's bound to be in the maser beam."

"They'll be ready this way."

"I wonder. I wish I could have warned them about the helmet. The very worst thing I can think of is that *Garner* might get his hands on the damn thing. Well, Lew's bright, he'll think of that himself."

Later he called Ceres again, to find out how the other side of the check was going. For more than two weeks now, Belt ships had been stopping and searching Earth ships at random. If Garner's snark hunt was an attempt to cover something, it wasn't going to work! But Ceres reported no results to date.

Ceres was wrong. The search-and-seizure tactics had had at least one result. Tension had never been so high between Earth and Belt.

The copilot sat motionless listening to Kzanol/Greenberg's side of the conversation. He couldn't understand overspeak, but Kzanol/Greenberg could; and Kzanol listened to the shielded slave through the mind of the copilot.

"I ought to get rid of you right away," Kzanol mused. "A slave that can't be controlled can't be trusted."

"That's truer than you know." A hint of bitterness showed in Kzanol/Greenberg's voice. "But you can't kill me yet. I have some information that you need very badly."

"So? What information?"

134

"I know where the second suit is. I also know why we weren't picked up, and I've figured out where the rrgh—where our race is now."

Kzanol said, "I think I also know where the second suit is. But for whatever else you may know, I won't kill you."

"Big of you." Kzanol/Greenberg waved the disintegrator negligently. "I'll tell you something you can't use first, to prove I know my stuff. Did you know white-foods were intelligent?"

"Whitefood droppings."

"Humans have found them on Sirius A-III-1. They're definitely whitefoods. They're also definitely sentient. Can you think of any way they could have developed intelligence?"

"No."

"Of course not. If any form of life has ever been mutation-proof, it's the whitefoods. Besides, what does a herbivore with no manipulatory appendages, and no natural defenses except sentient herders to kill off natural enemies, want with intelligence? No, the tnuctipun must have made them sentient in the first place. Making the brains a delicacy was just an excuse for making them large."

Kzanol sat down. His mouth tendrils stood straight out, as if he were smelling with them. "Why should they do that?"

He was hooked.

"Let me give it to you all in one bundle," said Kzanol/Greenberg. He took off his helmet and sat, found and lighted a cigarette, taking his time, while Kzanol grew silently but visibly enraged. There was no reason why the thrint shouldn't get angry, Kzanol/Greenberg thought, as long as he didn't get *too* angry.

"All right," he began. "First point is that the white-foods are sentient. Second point, you remember that there was a depression when Plorn's tnuctipun came up with antigravity."

"Powerloss, yes," Kzanol said fervently—and untactfully. "He should have been assassinated right away."

"Not him. His tnuctipun. Don't you see? They were fighting an undeclared war even then. The free tnuctipun must have been behind it all the time: the tnuctip fleet that escaped into space when Thrintun found the tnuctip system. They didn't try to reach Andromeda. They must have stayed between the stars, where nobody ever goes . . . went. A few civilized tnuctip must have taken their orders. The whitefoods were their spies; every noble in the galaxy, everyone who could afford to, used to keep whitefoods on his land."

"You're a ptavv fool. You're basing all these suppositions on the idiotic idea that whitefoods are intelligent. That's nonsense. We'd have sensed it."

"No. Check with Masney if you don't believe me. Somehow the tnuctipun must have developed a whitefood brain that was immune to the Power. And that one fact makes it certain that the whole ploy was deliberate. The whitefood spies. The antigravity, released to cause a depression. There may have been other ideas, too. Mutated racing viprin were introduced a few years before antigravity. They put all the legitimate viprin ranches out of business. That started the depression, and antigravity sped it along. The sunflowers were usually the only defense for a plantation; and everyone who had land had a sunflower border. It got the landowners used to isolation and independence, so that they might not cooperate in wartime. I'd give odds the tnuctipun had a spray to kill sunflowers. When the depression was in full swing they struck."

Kzanol didn't speak. His expression was hard to read.

"This isn't all supposition. I've got solid facts. First, the bandersnatchi, whitefoods to us, are sentient. Humans aren't stupid. They wouldn't make a mistake like that. Second, it's a fact that you weren't picked up when you hit F124. Why?"

"That is an ingesting good question. Why?"

136

This was the starting point, the hurt that had rankled in Kzanol/Greenberg's breast for sixteen days of retrospection and introspection, sixteen days during which he had had nothing to do but supervise Masney and brood on his bad luck. His mind had followed a path that started with a brooding, silent bandersnatch and ended in a war fought aeons ago. But he could have missed it all, he might have been spared all this torment and danger, if only that fool of a caretaker had seen the flash. He had not, and there could be only one reason.

"Because there wasn't anyone on the Moon. Either the caretaker was killed in the revolt, or he was off fighting somewhere. Probably he was dead. The tnuctipun would have moved at once to cut off our food supply."

"To what?" Kzanol was clearly lost. Thrintun had never fought anything but other thrintun, and the last war had been fought before star travel. Kzanol knew nothing of war.

The thrint tried to get back to basics. "You said you could tell me where the thrintun are now."

"With the tnuctipun. They're dead, extinct. If they weren't dead they would have reached Earth by now. That goes for the tnuctipun too, and nearly every other species that served us. They must have all died in the war."

"But that's insane. Somebody has to win a war!"

He sounded so sincere that Kzanol/Greenberg laughed. "Not so. Ask any human. Ask a Russian or a Chinese. They'll think you're a fool for needing to ask, but they'll tell you all about Pyrrhic victory. Shall I tell you what may have happened?"

He didn't wait for an answer. "This is pure conjecture, but it makes sense to me, and I've had two weeks to think about it. We must have been losing the war. If we were, some thraargh—excuse me. Some members of our race must have decided to take all the slaves with them. Like Grandfather's funeral ceremony, but bigger. They made an amplifier helmet strong enough to blanket the entire galaxy. Then they ordered everything within reach to commit suicide."

"But that's a horrible attitude!" Kzanol bristled with moral outrage. "Why would a thrint do a thing like that?"

"Ask a human. He knows what sentients are capable of when someone threatens them with death. First they declaim that the whole thing is horribly immoral, and that it's unthinkable that such a threat would ever be carried out. Then they reveal that they have similar plans, better in every respect, and have had them for years, decades, centuries. You admit the Big Amplifier would have been technically feasible?"

"Of course."

"Do you doubt that a slave race in revolt would settle for nothing less than our total extinction?"

Tendrils writhed in battle at the corners of Kzanol's mouth. When he finally spoke, he said, "I don't doubt it."

"Then—"

"Certainly we'd take them with us into extinction! The sneaky, dishonorable lower-than-whitefoods, using our concessions of freedom to destroy us! I only desire that we got them all."

Kzanol/Greenberg grinned. "We must have. How else can we explain that *none* of our slaves are in evidence except whitefoods? Remember whitefoods are immune to the Power.

"Now, that other information. Have you looked for your second suit?"

Kzanol returned to the present. "Yes, on the moons. And you searched Neptune. I'd have known if Masney found it. Still, there's one more place I'd like to search."

"Go ahead. Let me know when you're finished."

Gyros hummed faintly as the *Golden Circle* swung around. Kzanol looked straight ahead, his Attention in the control room. Kzanol/Greenberg lit a cigarette and got ready for a wait.

If Kzanol had learned patience, so had his poor man's imitation. Otherwise he would have done something foolish when the thrint blithely took over Masney, his own personal slave. He could have killed the thrint merely for using his own body—Kzanol/Greenberg's own stolen body, by every test of memory. And the effort of dealing with Kzanol, face to his own personal face!

But he had no choice.

The remarkable thing was that he was succeeding. He faced a full-grown thrint on the thrint's own territory. He had gone a long way toward making Kzanol accept him as another thrint mind, a ptavv at least. Kzanol still might kill him; he wished that the thrint would pay more attention to the disintegrator! But he had done well so far. And was proud of it, which was all to the good. Kzanol/Greenberg's self-respect had been very low.

There was no more to be done now. He had better stay out of Kzanol's way for a while.

Kzanol's first move was to radar Kzanol/Greenberg's ship. When that failed to turn up the suit, Kzanol took over Masney again and made him search it from radar cone to exhaust cone, checking the assumption that the shielded slave had somehow sneaked the suit aboard and turned off the stasis field. He found nothing.

But the other seemed so sure of himself! Why, if he didn't have the suit?

They searched Triton again. Kzanol/Greenberg could see Kzanol's uncertainty growing as the search progressed. The suit wasn't on Neptune, wasn't on either moon, positively wasn't on the other ship, couldn't have stayed in orbit this long. Where was it?

The drive went off. Kzanol turned to face his tormentor, who suddenly felt as if his brain was being squeezed flat. Kzanol was giving it everything he had: screaming sense and gibberish, orders and rage and raw red hate, and question, question, question. The pilot moaned and covered his head. The copilot squealed, stood up and turned half around, and died with foam on her lips. She stood there beside the gaming table, dead, with only the magnets in her sandals to keep her from floating away. Kzanol/Greenberg faced the thrint as he would have faced a tornado.

The mental tornado ended. "Where is it?" asked Kzanol.

"Let's make a deal." Kzanol/Greenberg raised his voice so that the pilot could hear. In the corner of his eye he saw that the thrint had gotten the point: the pilot was coming in from the control bubble to take the co-pilot's place as translator.

Kzanol took out his variable-knife. He treated the disintegrator with supreme disregard. Perhaps he didn't think of it as a weapon. In any case, nothing uses a weapon on a thrint except another thrint. He opened the variable-knife to eight feet and stood ready to wave the invisibly thin blade through the rebellious sentient's body.

"I dare you," said Kzanol/Greenberg. He didn't bother to raise the disintegrator.

GET OUT, Kzanol told the pilot. Kzanol/Greenberg could have shouted. He'd won! Slaves may not be present at a battle, or a squabble, between thrint and thrint.

The pilot moved slowly toward the airlock. Too slowly. Either some motor area had been burned out in the mind fight, or the slave was reluctant to leave. Kzanol probed.

ALL RIGHT. BUT HURRY.

Very quickly, the pilot climbed into his spacesuit before leaving. The family of Racarliw had never mistreated a slave. . . .

The airlock door swung shut. Kzanol asked, "What kind of deal?"

He couldn't understand the answer. Feeling disgusted with himself, he said, "We'll have to turn on the radio. Ah, here it is." He bent his face against the wall so that a pair of eating tendrils could reach into the recess and flip a switch. Now the pilot could hear Kzanol/Greenberg speaking through his suit radio.

It never occurred to either that they were circling Robin Hood's barn. The slave *couldn't* be present in person.

"I repeat," said Kzanol. "What kind of deal?"

"I want a partnership share in control of Earth. Our agreement is not to be invalidated if we find other, uh, beings like you, or a government of same. Half to you, half to me, and your full help in building me an amplifier. You'd better have the first helmet; it might not fit my brain. I want your oath, your . . . Wait a minute, I can't pronounce it." He picked up a bridge sheet and wrote, "prtuuvl," in the dots and curlicues of over-speak. "I want you to swear by that oath that you will protect my half ownership to the best of your ability, and that you will never willingly jeopardize my life or my health, provided that I take you to where you can find the second suit. Swear also that we'll get humans to build me another amplifier, once we get back."

Kzanol thought for a full minute. His mental shield was as solid as the door on a lunar fort, but Kzanol/Greenberg could guess his thoughts well enough. He was stalling for effect. Certainly he had decided to give the oath; for the prtuuvl oath was binding between thrint and thrint. Kzanol need only regard him as a slave . . .

"All right," said Kzanol. And he gave the prtuuvl oath without missing a single syllable.

"Good," Kzanol/Greenberg approved. "Now swear to the same conditions, by *this* oath." He pulled a bridge sheet from his breast pocket and passed it over. Kzanol took it and looked.

"You want me to swear a kpitlithtulm oath *too*?"

"Yes." There was no need to spell it out for Kzanol, nor even to repress his dolphin grin. The kpitlithtulm oath was for use between thrint and slave. If he swore the kpitlithtulm oath and the prtuuvl oath he would be committed for keeps, unless he chose to regard Kzanol/Greenberg as a plant or a dumb animal. Which would be dishonorable.

Kzanol dropped the paper. His mind shield was almost flickering, it was so rigid. Then his jaws opened wide and his lips pulled back from the needle fangs in a smile more terrible than *Tyrranosaurus rex* chasing a paleontologist, or Lucas Garner hearing a good joke. Seeing Kzanol, who could doubt that this was a carnivore? A ravenous carnivore which intended to be fed at any moment. One might forget that Kzanol was half the weight of a man, and see instead that he was larger than one hundred scorpions or three wildcats or a horde of marching soldier ants or a school of piranha.

But Kzanol/Greenberg recognized it as a smile of rueful admiration, a laughing surrender to a superior adversary, the smile of a good loser. With his thrint memories he saw further than that. Kzanol's smile was as phony as a brass transistor.

Kzanol gave the oath four times, and made four invalidating technical mistakes. The fifth time he gave up and swore according to protocol.

"All right," said Kzanol/Greenberg. "Have the pilot take us to Pluto."

"A-a-all right, everybody turn ship and head for three, eighty-four, twenty-one." The man in the lead ship sounded wearily patient. "I don't know what the game is, but we can play just as good as any kid on the block."

"Pluto," said someone. "He's going to Pluto!" He seemed to take it as a personal affront.

Old Smoky Petropoulos thumbed the transmitter. "Lew, hadn't one of us better stop and find out what's with the other two ships?"

"Uh. Okay, Smoky, you do it. Can you find us later with a maser?"

"Sure, boss. No secrets?"

"Hell, they know we're following them. Tell us anything we need to know. And find out where Garner is! If he's in the honeymooner I want to know it. Better

142

beam Woody in Number Six too, and tell him to go wherever Garner is."

"Of course, Pluto. Don't you get it yet?" It was not the first time Kzanol/Greenberg had had doubts about his former self's intelligence. The doubts were getting hard to ignore. He'd been afraid Kzanol would figure it out for himself. But—?

"No," said Kzanol, glowering.

"The ship hit one of Neptune's moons," Kzanol/Greenberg explained patiently, "so hard that the moon was smacked out of orbit. The ship was moving at nearly lightspeed. The moon picked up enough energy to become a planet, but it was left with an eccentric orbit which still takes it inside Neptune at times. Naturally that made it easy to spot."

"I was told that Pluto came from another solar system."

"So was I. But it doesn't make sense. If that mass dived into the system from outside, why didn't it go back out again to complete the hyperbola? What could have stopped it? Well, I'm taking a gamble.

"There's only one thing that bothers me. Pluto isn't very big. Do you suppose the suit may have been blown back into space by the explosion when it hit?"

"If it was, I'll kill you," said Kzanol.

"Don't tell me, let me guess," begged Garner. "Aha! I've got it. Smoky Petropoulos. How are you?"

"Not as good as your memory. It's been a good twenty-two years." Smoky stood behind the two seats, in the airlock space, and grinned at the windshield reflection of the two men. There wasn't room to do much else. "How the hell are you, Garner? Why don't you turn around and shake hands with an old buddy?"

"I can't, Smoky. We've been ordered not to move by a BEM that doesn't take no for an answer. Maybe a good hypnotherapist could get us out of this fix, but we'll have to wait 'til then. By the way, meet Leroy Anderson."

"Hi."

"Now give us a couple of cigarettes, Smoky, and put them in the corners of our mouths so we can talk. Are your boys chasing Greenberg and the BEM?"

"Yeah." Smoky fumbled with cigarettes and a lighter. "Just what is this game of musical chairs?"

"What do you mean?"

Old Smoky put their cigarettes where they belonged. He said, "That honeymoon special took off for Pluto. Why?"

"Pluto!"

"Surprised?"

"It wasn't here," said Anderson.

"Right," said Garner. "We know what they're after, and we know now they didn't find it here. But I can't imagine why they think it's on Pluto. Oops! Hold it." Garner puffed furiously at his cigarette: good honest tobacco with the tars and nicotine still in it. He didn't seem to have any trouble moving his face. "Pluto may have been a moon of Neptune once. Maybe that has something to do with it. How about Greenberg's ship? Is it going in the same direction?"

"Uh uh. Wherever it is, its drive is off. We lost sight of it four hours ago."

Anderson spoke up. "If your friend is still aboard he could be in trouble."

"Right," said Garner. "Smoky, that ship could be falling into Neptune with Lloyd Masney aboard. You remember him? A big, stocky guy with a mustache."

"I think so. Is he paralyzed too?"

"He's hypnotized. Plain old garden-variety hypnotized, and if he hasn't been told to save himself, he won't. Will you?"

"Sure. I'll bring him back here." Smoky turned to the airlock.

"Hey!" Garner yelped. "Take the butts out of our mouths before our faces catch fire!"

From his own ship Smoky called Woody Atwood in Number Six, the radar proof, and told his story. "It looks like the truth, Woody," he finished. "But there's no point in taking chances. You get in here and stick close to Garner's ship; if he makes a single move he's a bloody liar, so keep an eye open. He's been known to be tricky. I'll see if Masney is really in trouble. He shouldn't be hard to find."

"Pluto's a week and a half away at one gravity," said Anderson, who could do simple computations in his head. "But we couldn't follow that gang even if we could move. We don't have the fuel."

"We could refuel on Titan, couldn't we? Where the hell is Smoky?"

"Better not expect him back today."

Garner growled at him. Space, free fall, paralysis, and defeat were all wearing away at his self-control.

"Hey," he whispered suddenly.

"What?" The word came in an exaggerated stage whisper.

"I can wiggle my index fingers," Garner snapped. "This hex may be wearing off. And mind your manners."

Smoky was back late the next day. He had inserted the pointed nose of his ship into Masney's drive tube to push Masney's ship. When he turned off his own drive the two ships tumbled freely. Smoky moved between ships with a jet pack in the small of his back. By this time Atwood had joined the little group, and was helping Smoky, for it would have been foolish to suspect trickery after finding Masney.

Not because Masney was still hypnotized. He wasn't. Kzanol had freed him from hypnosis in the process of taking him over, and had, kindly or thoughtlessly, left him with no orders when he departed for Pluto. But Masney was near starvation. His face bore deep wrinkles of excess skin, and the skin of his torso was a loose,

145

floppy, folded tent over his ribcage. Kzanol/Greenberg had repeatedly forgotten to feed him, remembering only when hunger seemed about to break him out of hypnosis. Kzanol would never have treated a slave that way; but Kzanol, the real Kzanol, was far more telepathic than the false. And—Kzanol/Greenberg hadn't learned to think of daily food intake as a necessity. So much food was a luxury, and a foolish one.

Masney had started an eating spree as soon as the *Golden Circle* was gone, but it would be some time before he was "stocky" again. His ship's fuel was gone, and he was found drifting in a highly eccentric orbit about Triton, an orbit which was gradually narrowing.

"Couldn't possibly be faked," Smoky said when he called the Belt fleet. "A little bit better fakery, and Masney would be dead. As it is, he's only very sick."

Now the four ships fell near Nereid.

"We've got to refuel all these ships," said Garner. "And there's a way to do it." He began to tell them.

Smoky howled. "I won't leave my ship!"

"Sorry, Smoky. See if you can follow this. We've got three pilots, right? You, Woody, Masney. Me and Anderson can't move. But we've got four ships to pilot. We have to leave one."

"Sure, but why mine?"

"Five men to carry in three ships. That means we keep both two-man ships. Right?"

"Right."

"We give up your ship, or we give up a radar proof ship. Which would you leave?"

"You don't think we'll get to Pluto in time for the war?"

"We might as well try. Want to go home?"

"All right, all right."

The fleet moved to Triton without Number Four, and with half of Number Four's fuel transferred to Masney's ship, the *Iwo Jima*. Garner was Masney's passenger, and Smoky was in the *Heinlein* with Anderson. The three ships hovered over the big moon's icy surface while their drives melted through layer after layer of frozen gases, nitrogen and oxygen and carbon dioxide, until they reached the thick water ice layer. They landed on water ice, each in its own shallow cone. Then Woody and Smoky went after Number Four.

Smoky brought the singleship down with its tank nearly empty. They drained what was left into the *Iwo Jima,* and followed it with the *Heinlein*'s supply. Woody turned off the cooling unit in the singleship's hydrogen tank, dismantled the heater in the cabin and moved it into the tank. He had to cut a hole in the wall to get in.

The next few hours were spent cutting blocks of water ice. Masney was still convalescing, so the Belters had to do all the work. When they broke off they were exhausted, and two laser cutting tools were near death; but Number Four's fuel tank was filled with warm, not very clean water.

They hooked up the battery from Number Six to electrolyze the melted ice. Hydrogen and oxygen, mixed, poured into the *Heinlein*'s tank. They set the thermostat above the condensation point of hydrogen; but the oxygen fell as snow, and Smoky and Woody alternated positions in the bottom of the tank, shoveling the snow out. Once they had to take Number Six up and fly her around to recharge her batteries. Always there was the flavor of time passing, of the "war" leaving them further behind with each passing minute.

In two days they had fueled all three ships. The tanks were not full, but they would carry the little secondary fleet to Pluto, driving all the way, with fuel to spare. Number Four was useless, her tank clogged with dirt.

"We'll be three days late for whatever happens," Woody said glumly. "Why go at all?"

"We can stay close enough for radio contact," Smoky argued. "I'd like to have Garner close enough to tell the fleet what to do. He knows more about these Bug Eyed Monsters than any of us."

Luke said, "Main argument is that it may take the

fleet three days to lose. Then we get there and save the day. Or we don't. Let's go."

Woody Atwood masered the fleet immediately, knowing that the others could not intercept the conversation. If they had moved into the maser beam their radios would have blown sky high.

"Matchsticks!" Kzanol's voice dripped with thrintun contempt. "We might just as well be playing Patience." It was a strange thing to say, considering that he was losing.

"Tell you what," Kzanol/Greenberg suggested. "We could divide the Earth up now and play for people. We'd get about eight billion each to play with, with a few left over. In fact, we could agree right now that the Earth should be divided by two north-south great circle lines, leave it at that 'til we get back with the amplifier, and play with eight billion apiece."

"Sounds all right. Why north-south?"

"So we each get all the choices of climate there are. Why not?"

"Agreed." Kzanol dealt two cards face down and one up. "Seven stud," announced the pilot.

"Fold," said Kzanol/Greenberg, and watched Kzanol snarl and rake in the antes. "We should have brought Masney," he said. "It might be dangerous, not having a pilot."

"So? Assume I'd brought Masney. How would you feel, watching me operate your former slave?"

"Lousy." In point of fact, he now saw that Kzanol had shown rare tact in leaving Masney behind. Lloyd was a used slave, one who had been owned by another. Tradition almost demanded his death, and certainly decreed that he must never be owned by a self-respecting thrint, though he might be given to a beggar.

"Five stud," said the pilot. He sat where he could see neither hand, ready to wrap his human tongue around human, untranslatable poker slang when Kzanol wished to speak, and ready to translate for Kzanol/Greenberg. Kzanol dealt one up, one down.

"That's funny," said Kzanol/Greenberg. "I almost remembered something, but then it slipped away."

"Open your mind and I'll tell you what it was."

"No. It's in English anyway. From the Greenberg memories." He clutched his head. "What is it? It seems so damned appropriate. Something about Masney."

"Play."

"Nine people."

"Raise five."

"Up ten."

"Call. Greenberg, why is it that you win more than I do, even though you fold more often?"

Kzanol/Greenberg snapped his fingers. "Got it! 'When I am grown to man's estate I shall be very proud and great. And tell the other girls and boys Not to meddle with my toys.' Stevenson." He laughed. "Now what made me . . ."

"Deuce for you, queen for me," said the pilot. Kzanol continued in thrintun: "If men had telepathic recorders they wouldn't have to meddle with sounds that way. It has a nice beat, though."

"Sure," Kzanol/Greenberg said absently. He lost that hand, betting almost two hundred on a pair of fours.

Somewhat later Kzanol looked up from the game. "Communicator," he said. He got up and went to the pilot room. Kzanol/Greenberg followed. They took seats next to the control room door and the pilot turned up the volume.

". . . Atwood in Number Six. I hope you're listening, Lew. There is definitely an ET on the honeymooner, and he definitely has wild talents. There's nothing phony about any of this. The alien paralyzed the Arm and his chauffeur from a distance of around a million miles. He's pretty callous, too. The man in the second ship was left drifting near Triton, half starved and without fuel, after the alien was through with him. Garner says Greenberg

149

was responsible. Greenberg's the one who thinks he's another ET. He's on the honeymooner now. There are two others on the honeymooner, the pilot and copilot. Garner says shoot on sight, don't try to approach the ship. I leave that to you. We're three days behind you, but we're coming anyway. Number Four is on Triton, without fuel, and we can't use it until we clean the mud out of the tank. Only three of us can fly. Garner and his chauffeur are still paralyzed, though it's wearing off a little. We should have a hypnotherapist for these flatlanders, or they may never dance again.

"In my opinion your first target is the amplifier, if you can find it. It's far more dangerous than any single ET. The Belt wouldn't want it except for research, and I know some scientists who'd hate us for giving up *that* opportunity, but you can imagine what Earth might do with an amplifier for telepathic hypnosis.

"I'm putting this on repeat.

"Lew, this is Atwood in Number Six. Repeat, Atwood in . . ."

Kzanol/Greenberg pulled a cigarette and lit it. The honeymooner had a wide selection; this one was double filtered, mentholated, and made from de-nicotinized tobaccos. It smelled like gently burning leaves and tasted like a cough drop. "Shoot on sight," he repeated. "That's not good."

The thrint regarded him with undisguised contempt. To fear a slave—! But then, it was only a ptavv itself.

Kzanol/Greenberg glared. He knew more about people than Kzanol did, after all!

"All ships," said the man in the lead ship. "I say we shoot now. Comments?"

There were comments. Lew waited them out, and then he spoke.

"Tartov, your humanitarian impulses do you credit. No sarcasm intended. But things are too sticky to worry about two flatlanders in a honeymoon special. As for find-ing the amplifier, I don't think we have to worry about that. Earth won't find it before we do. They don't know what we know about Pluto. We can post guard over the planet until the Belt sends us an automatic orbital guard-ian. Radar may show us the amplifier; in that case we drop a bomb on it, and the hell with the research pos-sibilities. Have I overlooked anything?"

A feminine voice said, "Send one missile with a cam-era. We don't want to use up all our firepower at once."

"Good, Mabe. Have you got a camera missile?"

"Yes."

"Use it."

The *Iwo Jima* had been a week out from Earth, and Kzanol/Greenberg had been daydreaming, as usual. For some reason he'd remembered his watch: the formal el-bow watch with the cryogenic gears, now buried in the second suit. He'd have to make a new band.

But what for? It always ran slow. He'd had to adjust it every time he came back from a visit. . . . From a visit to another plantation. From a trip through space.

But of course. Relativity had jinxed his watch. Why hadn't he seen that before?

Because he'd been a thrint?

"Raise thirty," said Kzanol. He had a five down to match his pair showing, and it wasn't that he thought Kzanol/Greenberg was bluffing, with his four-straight showing. He hadn't noticed that the numbers were in se-quence.

Stupid. Thrintun were stupid. Kzanol couldn't play poker even when drawing on the pilot's knowledge. He hadn't guessed that his ship must have hit Pluto. He didn't need brains; he had the Power.

Thrintun hadn't needed intelligence since they'd found their first slave race. Before, the Power hadn't mattered; there was nothing to use it on. With an unlimited supply of servants to do their thinking, was it any wonder if they had degenerated?

"Raise fifty," said Kzanol/Greenberg. The thrint smiled.

⚮

"I never thought the Arms was a grand idea," said Luke. "I think they're *necessary*. Absolutely necessary. I joined because I thought I could be useful."

"Luke, if flatlanders need thought police to keep them alive, they shouldn't stay alive. You're trying to hold back evolution."

"We are not thought police! What we police is technology. If someone builds something that has a good chance of wiping out civilization, then and only then do we suppress it. You'd be surprised how often it happens."

Smoky's voice was ripe with scorn. "Would I? Why not suppress the fusion tube while you're at it? No, don't interrupt me, Luke, this is important. They don't use fusion only in ships. Half Earth's drinking water comes from seawater distilleries, and they all use fusion heat. Most of Earth's electricity is fusion, and all of the Belt's. There's fusion flame in crematoriums and garbage disposal plants. Look at all the uranium you have to import, just to squirt into fusion tubes as primer! And there are hundreds of thousands of fusion ships, every last one of which—"

"—turns into a hydrogen bomb at the flip of a switch."

"Too right. So why doesn't the Arms suppress fusion?"

"First, because the Arms was formed too late. Fusion was already here. Second, because we need fusion. The fusion tube *is* human civilization, the way the electrical generator used to be. Thirdly, because we won't interfere with anything that helps space travel. But I'm glad—"

"You're begging the—"

"MY TURN, Smoky. I'm glad you brought up fusion, because that's the whole point. The purpose of the Arms is to keep the balance wheel on civilization. Knock that balance wheel off kilter, and the first thing that would happen would be war. It always is. This time it'd be the last. Can you imagine a full-scale war, with that many hydrogen bombs just waiting to be used? Flip of a switch, I think you said."

"You said. Do you have to stamp on human ingenuity to keep the balance wheel straight? That's a blistering condemnation of Earth, if true."

"Smoky, if it weren't top secret I could show you a suppressed projector that can damp a fusion shield from ten miles away. Chick Watson got to be my boss by spotting an invention that would have forced us to make murder legal. There was—"

"Don't tell me about evidence you can't produce."

"All right, dammit, what about this amplifier we're all chasing? Suppose some bright boy came up with an amplifier for telepathic hypnosis? Would you suppress it?"

"You produce it and I'll answer."

Masney said, "Oh, for Christ's sake, you two!"

"Dead right," Anderson's voice answered. "Give us innocent bystanders an hour's rest."

The man in the lead ship opened his eyes. Afterimages like pastel amoebae blocked his vision; but the screen was dark and flat. "All ships," he said. "We can't shoot yet. We'll have to wait 'til they turn around."

Nobody questioned him. They had all watched through the camera in its nose as Mabe Doolin's test missile approached the *Golden Circle*. They had watched the glare of the honeymooner's drive become blinding, even with the camera picture turned all the way down. Then the

153

screens had gone blank. The fusing hydrogen turned missiles to molten slag before they could get close.

The honeymooner was safe for another day.

Kzanol/Greenberg reached a decision. "Hold the fort," he said. "I'll be right back."

Kzanol watched him get up and pull on his space suit. "What are you doing?"

"Slowing down the opposition, if I'm lucky." The near-ptavv went up the ladder into the airlock.

Kzanol sighed, pocketed the one-man matchsticks of the ante, and shuffled for solitaire. He knew that the slave with the ptavv mind was making a tremendous fuss over nothing. Perhaps it had brooded too long on the hypothetical tnuctip revolt, until all slaves looked dangerous.

Kzanol/Greenberg emerged on the dorsal surface of the hull. There were a number of good reasons for putting the airlock there, the best being that men could walk on the hull while the drive was on. He put his magnetic sandals on, because it would be a long fall if he slipped, and walked quickly aft to the tail. A switch buried in the vertical fin released a line of steps leading down the curve of the hull to the wing. He climbed down. The hydrogen light was terribly bright; even with his eyes covered he could feel the heat on his face. When he knelt on the trailing edge the wing shielded him from the light.

He peered over the edge. If he leaned too far he would be blinded, but he had to go far enough to see . . . Yes, there they were. Five points of light, equally bright, all the same color. Kzanol/Greenberg dropped the nose of the disintegrator over the edge and pulled the trigger.

If the disintegrator had had a maser type of beam, it could have done some real damage. But then, he could never have hit any of those tiny targets with such a narrow beam. Still, the cone spread too rapidly. Kzanol/Greenberg couldn't see any effect. He hadn't really expected to. He held the digger pointed as best he could at the five clustered stars. Minutes ticked by.

"What the hell . . . Lew! Are we in a dust cloud?"

"No." The man in the lead ship looked anxiously at the frosted quartz of his windshield. "Not that our instruments can tell. This may be the weapon Garner told us about. Does everyone have a messed-up windshield?"

A chorus of affirmatives.

"Huh! Okay. We don't know how much power there is in that machine, but it may have a limit. Here's what we'll do. First, we let the instruments carry us for a while. Second, we're eventually going to break our windshields so we can see out, so we'll be going the rest of the way in closed suits. But we can't do that yet! Otherwise our faceplates will frost up. Third point." He glared around for emphasis, though nobody saw him. "Nobody go outside for any reason! For all we know, that gun can peel our suits right off our backs in ten seconds. Any other suggestions?"

There were.

"Call Garner and ask him for ideas." Mabel Doolin in Number Two did that.

"Withdraw our radar antennae for a few hours. Otherwise they'll disappear." They did. The ships flew on, blind.

"We need something to tell us how far this gun has dug into our ships." But nobody could think of anything better than "Go look later."

Every minute someone tested the barrage with a piece of quartz. The barrage stopped fifteen minutes after it had started. Two minutes later it started again, and Tartov, who was out inspecting the damage, scrambled into his ship with his faceplate opaqued along the right side.

Kzanol looked up to see his "partner" climbing wearily down through the airlock. "Very good," he said. "Has it occurred to you that we may need the disintegrator to dig up the spare suit?"

155

"Yeah, it has. That's why I didn't use it any longer than I did." In fact he'd quit because he was tired, but he knew Kzanol was right. Twenty-five minutes of almost continuous operation was a heavy drain on the battery. "I thought I could do them some damage. I don't know whether I did or not."

"Will you relax? If they get too close I'll take them and get us some extra ships and body servants."

"I'm sure of that. But they don't have to get that close."

The gap between the *Golden Circle* and the Belt fleet closed slowly. They would reach Pluto at about the same time, eleven days after the honeymooner left Neptune.

"There she goes," said somebody.

"Right," said Lew. "Everyone ready to fire?"

Nobody answered. The flame of the honeymooner's drive stretched miles into space, a long, thin line of bluish white in a faint conical envelope. Slowly it began to contract.

"Fire," said Lew, and pushed a red button. It had a tiny protective hatch over it, now unlocked. With a key.

Five missiles streaked away, dwindling match flames. The honeymooner's fire had contracted to a point.

Minutes passed. An hour. Two.

The radio beeped. "Garner calling. You haven't called. Hasn't anything happened yet?"

"No," said Lew into the separate maser mike. "They should have hit by now."

Minutes dragging by. The white star of the honeymoon special burned serenely.

"Then something's wrong." Garner's voice had crossed the light-minutes between him and the fleet. "Maybe the disintegrator burned off the radar antennae on your missiles."

"Son of a bitch! Sure, that's exactly what happened. Now what?"

Minutes.

"Our missiles are okay. If we can get close enough we

156

can use them. But that gives them three days to find the amplifier. Can you think of a way to hold them off for three days?"

"Yeah." Lew was grim. "I've an idea they won't be landing on Pluto." He gnawed his lip, wondering if he could avoid giving Garner this information. Well, it wasn't exactly top secret, and the Arm would probably find out anyway. "The Belt has made trips to Pluto, but we never tried to land there. Not after the first ship took a close-up spectroscopic reading . . ."

They played at a table just outside the pilot room door. Kzanol/Greenberg had insisted. He played with one ear cocked at the radio. Which was all right with Kzanol, since it affected the other's playing.

Garner's voice came, scratchy and slightly distorted, after minutes of silence. "It sounds to me as if it all depends on where they land. We can't control that. We'd better think of something else, just in case. What have you got besides missiles?"

The radio buzzed gently with star static.

"I wish we could hear both sides," Kzanol growled. "Can you make any sense of that?"

Kzanol/Greenberg shook his head. "We won't, either. They must know we're in Garner's maser beam. But it sounds like they know something we don't."

"Four."

"I'm taking two. Anyway, it's nice to know they can't shoot at us."

"Yes. Well done." Kzanol spoke with absent-minded authority, using the conventional overspeak phrase to congratulate a slave who shows proper initiative. His eye was on his cards. He never saw the killing rage in his partner's face. He never sensed the battle that raged across the table, as Kzanol/Greenberg's intelligence fought his fury until it turned cold. Kzanol might have died that day, howling as the disintegrator stripped away suit and skin and muscle, without ever knowing why.

Ten days, twenty-one hours since takeoff. The icy planet hung overhead, huge and dirty white, with the glaring highlight which had fooled early astronomers. From Earth, only that bright highlight is visible, actually evidence of Pluto's flat, almost polished surface, making the planet look very small and very dense.

"Pretty puny," said Kzanol.

"What did you expect of a moon?"

"There was F-28. Too heavy even for whitefoods."

"True. Mmph. Look at that big circle. Looks like a tremendous meteor crater, doesn't it?"

"Where? Oh, I see it." Kzanol listened. "That's it! Radar's got it cold. Powerloss," he added, looking at the radar telescope through the pilot's eyes, "you can almost see the *shape* of it. But we'll have to wait for the next circuit before we can land."

Slowly the big ship turned until its motor faced forward in its orbit.

The Belt fleet stayed a respectful distance away—very respectful, four million miles respectful. Without the telescopes Pluto barely showed a disc.

"Everybody guess a number," said Lew. "Between one and one hundred. When I get yours I'll tell you mine. Then we call Garner and let him pick. Whoever gets closest to Garner's number is It."

"Three." "Twenty-eight." "Seventy."

"Fifty. Okay, I'll call Garner." Lew changed to maser. "One calling Garner. One calling Garner. Garner, we've about decided what to do if he doesn't go down. None of our ship radars are damaged, so we'll just program one ship to aim at the honeymooner at top speed. We watch through the telescopes. When our ship gets close enough we blow the drive. We want you to pick a number between one and one hundred."

Seconds passing. Garner's fleet was closer now, nearing the end of its trip.

"This is Tartov in Number Three. He's going down."

"Garner here. I suggest we wait and use the radar

proof, if we can. It sounds like you're planning for one man to ride in somebody's airlock until he can reach the Belt. If so, wait for us; we may have room for an extra in one of the Earth ships. You still want a number? Fifty-five."

Lew swallowed. "Thanks, Garner." He turned off his maser-finder.

"Three again. You're saved by the bell, Lew. He's going down on the night side. In the predawn area. Couldn't be better. He may even land in the Crescent!"

Lew watched, his face pale, as the tiny light burned above Pluto's dim white surface. Garner must have forgotten that a singleship's control bubble was its own airlock; that it had to be evacuated whenever the pilot wanted to get out. Lew was glad the flatlander fleet had followed. He did not relish the idea of spending several weeks riding on the outside of a spaceship.

Kzanol/Greenberg swallowed, swallowed again. The low acceleration bothered him. He blamed it on his human body. He sat in a window seat with the crash web tightly fastened, looking out and down.

There was little to see. The ship had circled half the world, falling ever lower, but the only feature on an unchanging cue-ball surface had been the slow creep of the planetary shadow. Now the ship flew over the night side, and the only light was the dim light of the drive, dim at least when reflected from this height. And there was nothing to see at all . . . until now.

Something was rising on the eastern horizon, something a shade lighter than the black plain. An irregular line against the stars. Kzanol/Greenberg leaned forward as he began to realize just how big the range was, for it couldn't be anything but a mountain range. "What's that?" he wondered aloud.

"One hundredth diltun." Kzanol probed the pilot's mind. The pilot said, "Cott's Crescent. Frozen hydrogen piled up along the dawn side of the planet. As it rotates

159

into daylight the hydrogen boils off and then refreezes on the night side. Eventually it rotates back to here."

"Oh. Thanks."

Evanescent mountains of hydrogen snow, smooth and low, like a tray of differently sized snowballs dropped from a height. They rose gently before the slowing ship, rank behind rank, showing the tremendous breadth of the range. But they couldn't show its length. Kzanol/Greenberg could see only that the mountains stretched half around the horizon; but he could imagine them marching from pole to pole around the curve of the world. As they must. As they did.

The ship was almost down, hovering motionless a few miles west of the beginning rise of the Crescent. A pillar of fire licked a mile down to touch the surface. Where it touched, the surface disappeared. A channel like the bed of a river followed below the ship, fading into the darkness beyond the reach of the light.

The ship rode with nose tilted high; the fusion flame reached slightly forward. Gently, gently, one mile up, the *Golden Circle* slowed and stopped.

Where the flame touched, the surface disappeared. A wide, shallow crater formed below the descending ship. It deepened rapidly. A ring of fog formed, soft and white and opaque, thickening in the cold and the dark, closing in on the ship. Then there was nothing but the lighted fog and the crater and the licking fusion fire.

This was the most alien place. He had been wasting his life searching out the inhabited worlds of the galaxy; for never had they given him such a flavor of strangeness as came from this icy world, colder than . . . than the bottom of Dante's Hell.

"We'll be landing on the water ice layer," the pilot explained, just as if he'd been asked. He had. "The gas layers wouldn't hold us. But first we have to dig down."

Had *he* been searching for strangeness? Wasn't that a Greenberg thought slipping into his conscious mind? Yes.

This soul-satisfaction was the old Greenberg starlust; he had searched for wealth, only wealth.

The crater looked like an open pit mine now, with a sloping ring wall and then an almost flat rim and then another, deeper ring wall and . . . Kzanol/Greenberg looked down, grinning and squinting against the glare, trying to guess which layer was which gas. They had been drilling through a very thick blanket of ice, hundreds or thousands of feet thick. Perhaps it was nitrogen? Then the next layer, appearing now, would be oxygen.

The plain and the space above it exploded in flame.

"She blows!" Lew crowed, like a felon reprieved. A towering, twisting pillar of yellow and blue flame roared straight up out of the telescope, out of the pale plain where there had been the small white star of the *Golden Circle*. For a moment the star shone brightly through the flames. Then it was swamped, and the whole scope was fire. Lew dropped the magnification by a ten-factor to watch the fire spread. Then he had to drop it again. And again.

Pluto was on fire. For billions of years a thick blanket of relatively inert nitrogen ice had protected the highly reactive layers below. Meteors, as scarce out here as sperm whales in a goldfish bowl, inevitably buried themselves in the nitrogen layer. There had been no combustion on Pluto since Kzanol's spaceship smashed down from the stars. But now hydrogen vapor mixed with oxygen vapor, and they burned. Other elements burned too.

The fire spread outward in a circle. A strong, hot wind blew out and up into vacuum, fanning great sheets of flame over the boiling ices until raw oxygen was exposed. Then the fire dug deeper. There were raw metals below the thin sheet of water ice; and it was thin, nonexistent in places, for it had all formed when the spaceship struck, untold eons ago, when food yeast still ruled Earth. Sodium and calcium veins; even iron burns furiously in the presence of enough oxygen and enough heat. Or chlorine, or fluorine; both halogens were present, blowing off the top of Pluto's frozen atmosphere, some burning with hydrogen in the first sheets of flame. Raise the temperature enough and even oxygen and nitrogen will unite.

Lew watched his screen in single-minded concentration. He thought of his future great-great-grandchildren and wondered how he could possibly make them see this as he saw it now. Old and leathery and hairless and sedentary, he would tell those children: "I saw a world burning when I was young. . . ." He would never see anything as strange.

Pluto was a black disc almost covering his scope screen, with a cold highlight near the sunward arm. In that disc the broad ring of fire had almost become a great circle, with one arc crawling over the edge of the world. When it contracted on the other side of the world there would be an explosion such as could only be imagined. But in the center the ring was darkening to black, its fuel nearly burned out.

The coldest spot within the ring was the point where the fire had started.

The *Golden Circle* had gone straight up, ringing and shivering from the blast, with sheets of fire roaring past the wing and hull. Kzanol/Greenberg had the wind knocked out of him. Kzanol was just now recovering consciousness. The ship was not yet harmed. It certainly hadn't been harmed by the heat of combustion. The ship's underbelly was built to withstand fusion heat for weeks.

But the *pilot* was out of control. His reflexes had taken over at the instant the shock wave hit, and then his conscious mind . . . He found himself his own master for the first time in weeks, and he made his decision. He turned off the fuel feed. The drive couldn't possibly be started again. Kzanol raged and told him to die, and he did, but it was too late. The ship, deprived of power, bucked and swooped in the burning wind.

Kzanol/Greenberg cursed fluent and ancient English.

Below him a wall of fire tens of miles high retreated toward the horizon. The ship hadn't turned over; the gyros must still be working.

The buffeting from below eased as the firelight died. The ship began to fall.

Deliberately, reluctantly, Lew took his eyes off the screen and shook himself. Then he turned on the radio. "All ships," he said. "Drive to Pluto at max. We can watch the fireworks on the way. Tartov, program us a course to land us on the dawn side of whatever's left of Cott's Crescent. Hexter, you haven't done anything useful lately. Find Ceres with a maser so I can fill them in to date. Comments?"

"This is Tartov. Lew, for Pete's sake! The planet's on *fire*! How can we land?"

"We've got four million miles to drive. The fire should be out when we get there. Oh, all right, get us into an orbit, but you're still gonna program our landing."

"*I* think we ought to leave a ship in orbit. Just in *case*."

"All right, Mabe. We'll gamble for who stays up. More comments?"

Three men and a woman pushed buttons that squirted volatilized uranium into fusion tubes and followed it with hydrogen. A growing storm of neutrons produced fission which produced heat which produced fusion. Four bluewhite stars formed, very long and very thin. The bright ends swung toward Pluto. They began to move.

"That's that," Masney said wearily. "And a good thing, too. Do you suppose there ever was a telepathy amplifier?"

"I'm sure there *is*. And it's not over yet." Luke was flexing his fingers and looking worried. Pluto showed on the screen before him, with the edge of the fire a straight line creeping west to east. "Lloyd, why do you think I didn't want the Belt to beat us to Pluto? Why did we come after them, anyway? That amplifier is a new weapon! If the Belt takes it apart and makes one that humans can use, we could see the worst and most permanent dictatorship in history. It might never end at all."

Masney looked at the future Luke had painted and, judging by his expression, found it evil. Then he grinned. "They can't land. It's all right, Luke. They can't get down to the helmet with that fire going."

"That fire isn't burning any more where the honeymooner came down."

Masney looked. "Right. Is Pluto still explosive?"

"I don't know. There might still be pockets of unburned material. But they can go down if they want, regardless. All they have to do is land on the day side, where there's no hydrogen, and land so fast they don't burn through the nitrogen layer. They'd sink into it, of course, from heat leakage through the hulls, so they'd eventually have to dig their way out. But that's nothing. What counts is the hydrogen. Miss that and you probably won't start a fire.

"Now, they'll almost certainly go down for the amplifier as soon as the fire stops. We've got to destroy it before they get it. Or after."

"Take a look," said Lloyd.

Four bright points formed in a cluster on the screen. In seconds they had grown into lines a mile long, all pointing in the same direction.

"We've got some time," said Masney. "They're millions of miles from Pluto."

"Not far enough." Luke reached to close the intership circuit. "Calling *Heinlein*. Anderson, the Belt fleet just took off for Pluto from four million miles away. How long?"

"They started from rest?"

"Close enough."

"Lessee . . . mmmmmmmmmm . . . five hours ten

minutes, approx. No less, maybe more, depending on whether they're scared of the fire."

"How long for us?"

"Fifty-nine hours now."

"Thanks, Anderson." Luke turned off the radio. Strange, how Smoky had sat there without saying a word. In fact, he hadn't said much of anything lately.

With a chill, Luke realized that Smoky's thoughts must run very like his own. With the ET a dead issue, the question was: Who got the helmet? Belt or Earth? And Smoky wasn't about to trust Earth with it.

Larry Greenberg opened his eyes and saw darkness. It was cold. "The lights don't work," said a voice in his mind.

"Did we crash?"

"We did indeed. I can't imagine why we're still alive. GET UP."

Larry Greenberg got up and marched down the aisle between the passengers' seats. His muscles, bruised and aching, seemed to be acting by themselves. He went to the pilot seat, removed the pilot and sat down. His hands strapped him, then folded themselves into his lap. There he sat. Kzanol stood beside him, barely in the range of his peripheral vision.

"Comfortable?"

"Not quite," Larry confessed. "Could you leave one arm free for smoking?"

"Certainly." Larry found his left arm would obey him. He still couldn't move his eyes, though he could blink. He pulled a cigarette and lit it, moving by touch.

He thought, "It's a good thing I'm one of those people who can shave without a mirror."

Kzanol asked, "What does that have to do with anything?"

"It means I don't get uncoordinated without my eyes."

Kzanol stood watching him, a blurred mass at the edge

165

of sight. Larry knew what he wanted. He wouldn't do it; he wouldn't ask.

What did Kzanol look like? he wondered.

He looked like a thrint, of course. Larry could remember being Kzanol/Greenberg, and all he had seen was a smallish, handsome, somewhat undergroomed thrint. But when he'd walked past Kzanol on his way to the pilot room, his fleeting glimpse had found something terrifying, something one-eyed and scaly and iridescent green, with gray giant earthworms writhing at the corners of a mouth like a slash in a child's rubber ball, with sharply pointed metallic teeth, with oversized arms and huge three-fingered hands like mechanical grabs.

The thrintun voice was chilly, by its own standards. "Are you wondering about my oath?"

"Oaths. Yes, now that you mention it."

"You can no longer claim to be a thrint in a human body. You are not the being I gave my oath to."

"Oaths."

"I still want you to help me manage Earth."

Larry had no trouble understar.ding even the inflections in overspeak, and Kzanol, of course, could now read his mind. "But you'll manage me," said Larry.

"Yes, of course."

Larry raised his cigarette and tapped it with a fore-finger. The ash fell slower than mist past his gaze and disappeared from sight. "There's something I should tell you," he said.

"Condense it. My time is short; I have to find something."

"I don't think you should own the Earth any more. I'll stop you if I can."

Kzanol's eating tendrils were doing something strange. Larry couldn't see what it was. "You think like a slave. Not a ptavv, a slave. You have no conceivable reason to warn me."

"That's my problem."

"Quite. DON'T MOVE UNTIL I RETURN." The

command carried overtones of disgust. A dark blur that was Kzanol moved and vanished.

Alone in the pilot room, Larry listened to the clanking, squeaking, and mental cursing that meant Kzanol was searching for something. He heard when the thrint sharply ordered the pilot to return to life and show him AT ONCE where he'd hidden the contaminated portable radar. . . . The command, a mere explosion of frustration, stopped suddenly. So did the sounds of search.

Presently Larry heard the airlock chugging to itself.

The clerk was a middleman. It was his job to set priorities on messages sent into and received from deep space. At three in the morning he answered the ring of the outside phone.

"Hello, Arms Maser Transceiving Station," he said a little sleepily. It had been a dull night.

It was no longer dull. The small brunette who looked out of his screen was startlingly beautiful, especially to the man who saw her unexpectedly in the dead hours.

"Hello. I have a message for Lucas Garner. He's on the way to Neptune, I think."

"Lucas Garner? What—I mean, what's the message?"

"Tell him that my husband is back to normal, and he should take it into consideration. It's very important."

"And who is your husband?"

"Larry Greenberg. That's G-r-e-"

"Yes, I know. But he's beyond Neptune by now. Wouldn't Garner already know anything you know about Greenberg?"

"Not unless he's telepathic."

"Oh."

It was a tricky decision for a clerk. Maser messages cost like uranium, less because of the power needed and the wear and tear on the delicate machines than because of the difficulty of finding the target. But only Garner could decide whether an undependable "hunch" was important to him. The clerk risked his job and sent the message.

The fire had slowed now. Most of the unburned hydrogen had been blown before the fire, until it was congested into a cloud mass opposite on Pluto from the resting place of the *Golden Circle*. Around that cloud bank raged a hurricane of awesome proportions. Frozen rain poured out of the heavens in huge lens-shaped drops, hissing into the nitrogen snow. The layers above nitrogen were gone, vaporized, gas diluting the hydrogen which still poured in. On the borderline hydrogen burned fitfully with halogens, and even with nitrogen to form ammonia, but around most of the great circle the fires had gone out. Relatively small, isolated conflagrations ate their way toward the new center. The "hot" water ice continued to fall. When it had boiled the nitrogen away it would begin on the oxygen. And *then* there would be a fire.

At the center of the hurricane the ice stood like a tremendous Arizona butte. Even the halogens were still frozen across its flat top, thousands of square miles of fluorine ice with near-vacuum above. Coriolis effects held back the burning wind for a time.

On the other side of the world, Kzanol stepped out of the *Golden Circle*.

He turned once to look back. The honeymoon ship was flat on her belly. Her landing gear was retracted, and a wide, smooth crater was centered under the drive exhaust cone. Star-hot hydrogen had leaked from the fusion tube for some time after its fuel was cut off. The fuselage was twisted, though not broken. Her forward wings had been jarred open, and now hung broken from their sockets. One tip of the triangular major wing curled up where it had stabbed against rock-hard ice.

She was doomed, she was useless. Kzanol walked on.

The thrintun space suit was a marvelous assemblage of tools. No changes had been made in it for centuries before Kzanol's time, for the design had long been perfect, but for an unsuspected flaw in the emergency systems, and the naïve thrintun had never reached that level of sophistication which produces planned obsolescence. The temperature inside the suit was perfect, even a little warmer than in the ship.

But the suit could not compensate for the wearer's imagination. Kzanol felt the outer chill as his ship fell behind. Miles-thick blankets of nitrogen and oxygen snow had boiled away here, leaving bubbly permafrost which showed dark and deep green in the light of his helmet lamp. There was fog, too, not dense but very deep, a single bank that stretched halfway around the world. The fog narrowed his universe to a circular patch of bubbly ice.

Moving in great, easy flying hops, he reached the first rise of the crescent in forty minutes. It was six miles from the ship. The crescent was now a slightly higher rise of permafrost, scarred and pitted from the fire that had crossed it. Kzanol's portable radar, borrowed from the *Circle*'s lockers, showed his goal straight ahead at the limit of its range. About a mile ahead, and almost a thousand feet deep in permafrost.

Kzanol began to climb the slope.

"We're out of arrows," the man in Number Two ship said gloomily. He meant missiles. "How do we protect ourselves?"

Lew said, "We'll be on our way home before Garner comes within sniffing distance of Pluto. The best he can do is shoot at us as we pass. His arrows aren't good enough to hit us when we're moving that fast, except by accident. He knows it. He won't even try, because it might start the Last War."

"He may decide the stakes are high enough."

"Dammit, Tartov, what choice have we got? Garner must not be allowed to leave here with that amplifier! If he does, we'll see a period of slavery such as nobody has even dreamed of up to now," Lew exhaled noisily through his nostrils. "We've got to go down and destroy the thing by hand. Land on the dawn side and mount an expedition. Hexter, can you dismount a ship's radar so it'll still work?"

"Sure, Lew. But it'll take two men to carry it."

Tartov said, "You miss my point. Of course we've got to wreck the damn amplifier. But how can we prove to Garner that we *did* wreck it? *Why should he trust us?*"

Lew ran spatulate fingers through tangled cotton hair. "My apologies, Tartov. That's a damn good question. Comments?"

Kzanol aimed the disintegrator thirty degrees downward and flipped the firing switch.

The tunnel formed fast. Kzanol couldn't see how fast, for there was nothing but darkness inside after the first second. A minor hurricane blew out of the tunnel. He leaned against the wind as against a wall. In the narrow cone of the beam the "wind" was clear, but beyond the edge it was a dust storm. The wind was dust, too, icy dust torn to particles of two and three molecules each by the mutual repulsion of the nuclei.

After ten minutes Kzanol decided the tunnel must be getting too wide. The opening was less than a foot across; he used the disintegrator to enlarge it. Even when he turned off the digging tool he couldn't see very far into it.

After a moment he walked into the darkness.

With his left hand Larry reached out and shook the pilot's shoulder. Nothing. It was like a wax figure. He would probably have felt the same way. But the man's cheek was cool. He was not paralyzed, but dead.

Somewhere in the back of his mind was Judy. It was different from the way it had been in the past. Now, he believed it. Even when separated by over three billion miles, he and Judy were somehow aware of each other. But no more than that.

He couldn't tell her anything. He couldn't warn her that

the Bug Eyed Whoosis was hours or minutes from owning the Earth.

The pilot couldn't help him. He had had an instant to make a choice, that professional hauler of millionaires, and he had made first a right choice and then a wrong one. He had decided to die, killing everyone aboard ship, and that was right. But he should have turned off the fusion shield, not the fuel feed! Now he was dead, and Kzanol was loose.

It was his fault. Without Larry Greenberg, Kzanol would have been blasted to gas when he made turnover for Pluto. He'd never have known the suit was on Pluto! The knowledge was galling.

Where was his mind shield? Two hours ago he had held an impenetrable telepathic wall, a shield that had stood up to Kzanol's most furious efforts. Now he couldn't remember how he'd done it. He was capable of it, he knew that, and if he could—hold it.

No, it was gone. Some memory, some thrintun memory.

Well, let's see. He'd been in Masney's office when the thrint had screamed at everybody to shut off their minds. His mind shield had—but it had already been there. Somehow he had already known how to use it. He had known ever since.

Sunflowers eight feet across. They turned round and round, following the sun as it circled the plantation at Kzathit's pole. Great silver paraboloid platters sending concentrated sunlight to their dark green photosynthetic nodes. Flexible mirrors mounted on thick bulging stalks, mirrors that could ripple gently to put the deadly focus wherever they wanted it: on a rebellious slave or a wild animal or an attacking enemy thrint. That focus was as deadly as a laser cannon, and the sunflowers never missed. For some reason they never attacked members of the House they protected.

In the grounded luxury liner, Larry Greenberg tingled. Fish on fire! The sunflowers must have been controlled by the tnuctipun house slaves! He had not the slightest

171

proof, but he knew. On a day in the past, every sunflower in the galaxy must have turned on its owner. . . . He thought, We thrintun—those thrintun really set themselves up. Suckers!

Remembering again, he saw that the sunflowers weren't as big as they looked. He was seeing them from Kzanol's viewpoint, Kzanol one and a half feet tall, a child of eight thrintun years. Kzanol half grown.

The maser beam reached for Pluto, spreading itself wide, dropping ever so slightly in frequency as it climbed out of the Sun's gravitational well. By the time it reached its target more than five hours had passed, and the wave front was a quarter of a million miles across.

Pluto didn't stop it. Pluto barely left a noticeable hole. There was enormous power behind this beam. The beam went on into the void, moving almost straight toward the galactic center, thinned by dust clouds and distance. It was picked up centuries later by beings who did not resemble humanity in the least. They were able to determine the shape of the conical beam, and to determine its apex. But not accurately enough.

In its wake—

Tartov said, "You were right, Lew. There's no fire where we're going."

"That's that, then. You three go on down. I'll warp into an orbit."

"We *really* ought to draw again, you know."

"Nuts, Mabe. Think how much I'll win at poker after using up all my bad luck out here. Got my orbit, Tartov?"

"Hook in your idiot savant and I'll give it the data direct."

"Autopilot on."

BEEP.

Lew felt his ship turning as the sound of the beep ended. The spears of fusion light alongside him began to dwindle in size. Could they manage without him? Sure, they were Belters. If danger came it would come here, in orbit. He said, "All ships. Good luck. Don't take any stupid chances."

"Hexter calling. Something on the Earth channel, Lew."

Lew used his frequency dial. "Can't find it."

"It's a little low."

"Oh. Typical. . . . Dammit, it's in code. Why should it be in code?"

"Maybe they've got little secrets," Tartov suggested. "Whatever it is, it's bound to be a good reason to finish this fast."

"Yeah. Look, you go ahead and land. I'll send this to Ceres for decoding. It'll take twelve hours to get an answer, but what the hell."

Why should it be in code?

Lit Shaeffer would have known.

Even now, sitting in his office deep in the rock of Ceres, with the bubble of Confinement winding its snail-slow orbit thirty miles overhead, Lit was preparing a note of apology to the United Nations. It was the hardest work he'd ever done! But there seemed no way out.

A week and a half ago there had been a maser message from Neptune. Garner's story was true: he had gone to Neptune in pursuit of a wildly dangerous ET. Lit had scowled and ordered an immediate end to the harassment of Earth shipping.

But the damage was done. For two weeks the Belt had persecuted Earth's meager shipping; had used codes in maser transmissions, even in solar weather forecasts, in violation of a century's tradition; had used their espionage network so heavily that its existence became insultingly obvious. Secretiveness and suspicion were the rule as never before. Earth had retaliated in kind.

Now the Belt had stopped using codes, but Earth had not.

Did the coded messages contain vital information? Almost certainly not, Lit would have guessed. Certain messages decoded at random bore him out. But the Belt couldn't be sure, which, of course, was the whole point.

And Belt ships were searched at Earth's ports, with insulting thoroughness.

This mistrust had to be stopped now. Lit gritted his teeth and continued writing.

The message started to repeat, and Lloyd switched it off with a decisive click.

"She felt him die," said Luke. "She didn't know it, but she felt him die."

His thoughts ran on without him. . . . She'd felt him die. What was it that let some people know things they couldn't possibly know? There seemed to be more and more of them lately. Luke had never been remotely psychic, and he'd envied the lucky few who could find lost rings or lost criminals without the slightest effort, with no more explanation than, "I thought you might have dropped it in the mayonnaise," or, "I had a hunch he was hiding in the subway, living off the tenth-mark peanut machines." Parapsychologists with their special cards had proven that psy powers exist; and had gone no further than that, in close to two hundred years, except for psionics devices like the contact machine. "Psionics," to Luke, meant "*I* don't know how the damn thing works."

How did Judy know that the *Golden Circle* had crashed? You couldn't know the answer, so you hung a tag on it. Telepathy.

"And even then," said Luke, not knowing that he spoke, "she managed to fool herself. Marvelous!"

"Did she?"

Luke's head jerked up and around. Lloyd was scared and not trying to hide it. He said, "The *Golden Circle* was a tough ship. Her drive was in her belly, remember? Her belly was built to stand fusion heat. And the explosion was *below* her."

Luke felt his own nerves thrill in sympathetic fear.

"We'll find out right now," he said, and touched the control panel. "All ships, listen in. Anderson, what do you know about the *Golden Circle*?"

"Yeah, I heard it too. It could be; it just could be. The people who built the honeymooners knew damn well that one accident or one breakdown could ruin a billion-mark business. They built the ships to stand up to anything. The *Golden Circle*'s life system is smaller in proportion than the life system of any ship here, just because they put so much extra weight in the walls and in the fail-safe systems."

In a dull voice, Smoky said, "And we're out of it."

"Hell we are. That message was in code. Lloyd, get the maser pointed at Pluto. We've got to warn the Belters. Smoky, is there a Mayday signal we can use?"

"No need. They'll hear you. It's too late anyway."

"What do you mean?"

"They're going down."

<hr>

Kzanol walked slowly through a tunnel which gleamed dull white where the light fell. With practice he had learned to stay the right distance behind the disappearing far wall, following his disintegrator beam, so that he walked in a sloppy cylinder six feet in diameter. The wind roared past him and ceased to be wind; it was flying dust and ice particles, flying in vacuum and low gravity, and it packed the tunnel solidly behind him.

The other suit was two hundred feet beyond the end of the sloping tube.

Kzanol looked up. He turned off the disintegrator and stood, stiffly furious, waiting. They had dared! They were just beyond control range, too far away and moving in fast, but they were decelerating as they closed in. He waited, ready to kill.

Mature consideration stopped him. He needed a ship in which to leave Pluto; his own was shot to heat death. Those above him were single seaters, useless to him, but he knew that other ships were coming. He must not frighten them away.

He would let these ships land.

Lew's singleship hung nose down over the surface of Pluto. He'd set the gyros that way. The ship would be nose down for a long time, perhaps until the gyros wore out. Yet he could see nothing. The planetary surface was hidden beneath a curtain of boiling storm clouds.

He knew that he had passed Cott's Crescent some minutes ago. He had heard the hum of an open intership circuit. Now, coming toward him over the curved horizon, was a storm within a storm: the titanic whirling hurricane he had passed over twice already. Pluto takes months to rotate. Only a monumental flow of air, air newly created, rushing around from the other side of the planet, could have carried enough lateral velocity to build such a sky whirlpool from mere Coriolis effects. Flames flickered in its roiling rim; but the center was a wide circle of calm, clear near-vacuum all the way down to the icy plateau.

Over the radio came the sound of Garner's voice.

". . . Please answer at once so we'll know you're all right. There is a real chance that the ET survived the crash, in which case—"

"Now you're telling me, you know-it-all son of a bitch!" Lew couldn't talk. His tongue and his lips were as frozen as the rest of his voluntary muscles. He heard the message all the way through, and he heard it repeated, and repeated. Garner sounded more urgent than he had ten minutes ago.

The hurricane was almost below him now. He looked straight down into the eye.

From one of the murky fires in the rim of the eye, a tongue reached inward.

It was like the first explosion, the one he'd watched through the telescope. But this wasn't the telescope! The whole plateau was lost in multicolored flame in the first twenty seconds. With the leisurely torpor of a sleepy ground sloth on a cold morning, the fire stood up and reached for him. It was fire and ice, chunks of ice big enough to see, ice burning as it rose in the clutch of the height and might, a blazing carnivore reaching to swallow him.

Viprin race. Bowed skeletal shapes like great albino whippets seemed to skim the dirt surface of the track, their jet nacelle nostrils flaring, their skins shining like oil, racing round and round the audience standing breathless in the center of the circle. The air was thick with Power: thousands of thrintun desperately hurling orders at their favorites, knowing perfectly well that the mutant viprin didn't have the brains to hear. Kzanol on one of the too-expensive seats, clutching a lavender plastic cord, knowing that this race, *this* race meant the difference between life as a prospector and life as a superintendent of cleaning machinery. He would leave here with commercials to buy a ship, or with none.

Larry dropped it. It was too late in Kzanol's life. He wanted to remember much earlier. But his brain seemed filled with fog, and the thrintun memories were fuzzy and hard to grasp. As Kzanol/Greenberg he had had no trouble with his memory, but as Larry he found it infuriatingly vague.

The earliest thing he could remember was that scene of the sunflowers.

He was out of cigarettes. The pilot might have some in his pocket, but Larry couldn't quite reach it. And he was hungry; he hadn't eaten in some ten hours. A gnal might help. Definitely one would help, for it would probably kill him in seconds. Larry tore a button from his shirt and put it in his mouth. It was round and smooth, very like a gnal.

He sucked it and let his mind dissolve.

Three ships rested on the other side of what remained of Cott's Crescent. In the control bubbles the pilots sat motionless, waiting for instructions and thinking furious, futile thoughts. In the fourth ship . . . Kzanol's eating tendrils stood away from his mouth as he probed.

It was rather like probing his own memory of the crash. A brightly burning wind, a universe of roaring, tearing flame and crushing shocks.

Well, it wasn't as if he *needed* Lew. Kzanol turned his disintegrator on and began walking. Something bright glimmered through the dark ice wall.

"They don't answer," said Lloyd.

Luke let himself sag against the constant one-gee deceleration. Too little, too late . . . the Belt was beaten. And then his eyes narrowed and he said, "They're bluffing."

Masney turned inquiringly.

"Sure. They're bluffing, Lloyd. They'd be fools not to. We handed them such a perfect chance! Like four spades up in a five stud hand. The perfect opportunity to get us fighting the wrong enemy."

"But we'd be getting this same scary silence if they were really caught."

Luke spoke jerky phrases as the answers came. "Right. We get quiet radios either way. But—we get the same answer either way, too. Shoot to kill. Either the fleet is on its way back with amplifier, or the ET has it and is on its way to conquer the Earth. Either way, we have to attack."

"You know what that means, don't you?"

"Tell me."

"We'll have to kill Atwood and Smoky first. And Anderson."

"O-o-oh. Right, about Atwood. He'd never let us

shoot at his friends, whether they're slaves or not. But we can hope Anderson can control Smoky."

"How's your coordination?"

"My—?" Luke pondered his uncertain, shaky hands and newly clumsy fingers, his lack of control over his sphincter muscles. Paralysis hangover. "Right again. Smoky'd make mincemeat of Anderson." A gusty sigh. "We'll have to blow both ships."

"Luke, I want a promise." Masney looked like Death. He was an old man in his own right, and he had been starved for some time. "I want you to swear that the first smell we get of the thought amplifier, we destroy it. Not capture, Luke. Destroy!"

"All right, Lloyd. I swear."

"If you try to take it home, I'll kill you. I mean it."

His finger, an oversized finger in an oversized mouth with tiny needle teeth. He was on his side, more a lump of flesh than anything else, and he sucked his finger because he was hungry. He would always be hungry.

Something huge came in, blocking light. Mother? Father. His own arm moved, jerking the finger contemptuously away, scraping it painfully on the new teeth. He tried to put it back, but it wouldn't move. Something forceful and heavy told him never to do that again. He never did.

No mind shield there. Funny, how sharp that picture was, the memory of early frustration.

Something . . .

The room was full of guests. He was four thrintun years old, and he was being allowed out for the first time. Shown proudly by his father. But the noise, the telepathic noise, was too loud. He was trying to think like everybody at once. It frightened him. Something terrible happened. A stream of dark brown semiliquid material shot out of his mouth and spread over the wall. He had defecated in public.

Rage, red and sharp. Suddenly he had no control over

his limbs; he was running, stumbling toward the door. Rage from his father and shame from himself—or from his father? He couldn't tell. But it hurt, and he fought it, closed his mind to it. Father went like a blown flame, and the guests too, and everybody was gone. He was all alone in an empty world. He stopped, frightened. The other minds came back.

His father was proud, proud! At the age of four little Kzanol already had the Power!

Larry grinned a predatory grin and got up. His vac suit—? In the lounge, on one of the seats. He got it and screwed it down and went out.

Kzanol tugged at the great bright bulk until it came out of the ice. It looked like a great crippled goblin lying on its back.

The ice had packed the tunnel solidly behind him; air tight, in fact. That was fortunate. Kzanol had used compressed air from his own suit to pressurize his icy chamber. He frowned at the dials on his upper chest, then took his helmet off.

The air was cold and thin. But now he needn't carry the amplifier helmet back to the ship. He could put it on here.

He looked down at the suit and realized that he'd want help getting it back. Kzanol turned his Attention to Larry Greenberg. He found a blank.

Greenberg was nowhere.

Had he died? No, surely Kzanol would have sensed that.

This wasn't good, not even a little bit good. Greenberg had warned him that he would try to stop him. The slave must be on his way now, with his mind shield in full working order. Fortunately the amplifier would stop him. It would control a full-grown thrint.

Kzanol reached down to turn the suit on its face. It was . . . not heavy, but massive . . . but it moved.

180

It was snowing. In the thin air the snow fell like gravel thrown by an explosion. It fell hard enough to kill an unprotected man. Where it hit it packed itself into a hard surface, just crunchy enough for good walking.

Luckily Greenberg didn't have to see. He could sense exactly where Kzanol was and he walked confidently in that direction. His suit wasn't as good as Kzanol's. The cold seeped gently through his gauntlets and boots. He'd suffered worse than this on skiing trips, and loved it.

Then the Power came lashing at his brain. His mind shield went up hard. The wave was gone in a moment. But now he couldn't find Kzanol. The thrint had put up his mind shield. Larry stopped, bewildered, then went on. He had a compass, so he would not walk in circles. But Kzanol must now know he was coming.

Gradually the afterimage pushed into his mind. In every sense, in eye and ears and touch and kinesthetic nerves, he felt what Kzanol had been doing when his Power lashed out.

He'd been bending over the second suit.

It was too late.

He couldn't run; the vac suit wasn't built for it. He looked around in a rising tide of desperation, and then, because there was no help for it, he walked on.

Walk. Knock the ice off your faceplate, and walk.

Walk until you're Told to stop.

Half an hour later, an hour after he'd left the ship, he began to see powdery snow. It was light and fluffy, very different from the falling icy bullets. It was the residue of Kzanol's digging. He could use it as a guide.

The powder snow grew deeper and deeper, until suddenly it reared as a towering mountain of packed snow. When he tried to climb it Larry kept slipping down the side in a flurry of snow. But he had to get up there! When Kzanol opened the suit it would be all over. He kept climbing.

He was halfway up, and nearly exhausted, when the top began to move. Snow shot out in a steady stream and fell in a slow fountain. Larry slid hastily down for fear of being buried alive.

The snow continued to pour out. Kzanol was digging his way back . . . but why wasn't he wearing the helmet?

The fountain rose higher. Particles of ice, frozen miles up in Pluto's burned and cooling atmosphere, pelted through the drifting fountain and plated itself on Larry's suit. He kept moving to keep his joints free. Now he wore a sheath of translucent ice, shattered and cracked at the joints.

And suddenly he guessed the answer. His lips pulled back in a smile of gentle happiness, and his dolphin sense of humor rose joyfully to the surface.

Kzanol climbed out of the tunnel, tugging the useless spare suit behind him. He'd had to use the disintegrator to clear away the snow in the tunnel, and he'd had to climb it at a thirty-degree rise, dragging a bulk as heavy as himself and wearing a space suit which weighed nearly as much. Kzanol was very tired. Had he been human, he would have wept.

The sight of the slope down was almost too much. Plow his feet through that stuff—? But he sighed and sent the spare suit rolling down the mountainside. He watched it hit the bottom and stay, half buried. And he followed it down.

The ice fell faster than ever, hundreds of thousands of tons of brand new water freezing and falling as the planet tried to regain its equilibrium state, forty degrees above absolute zero. Kzanol stumbled blind, putting one big chicken foot in front of the other and bracing for the jar as it fell, keeping his mind closed because he remembered that Greenberg was around somewhere. His mind was numb with fatigue and vicarious cold.

He was halfway down when the snow rose up and stood before him like a thrintun giant. He gasped and stopped moving. The figure slapped one mitten against its face-

182

plate and the thick ice shattered and fell. Greenberg! Kzanol raised the disintegrator.

Almost casually, with a smile that was purest dolphin, Larry reached out a stiff forefinger and planted it in Kzanol's chest.

∽◆∾

For thirty-four hours the singleship had circled Pluto, and it was too long by far. Garner and Masney had been taking turns sleeping so that they could watch the scope screen for the actinic streak of a singleship taking off. There had been little talk between the ships. What talk there was was a strain for all, for every one of the five men knew that battle was very close, and not one was willing even to hint at the possibility. Now Lew's single-ship showed in the scope screen even with its drive off. Now Luke, watching although it was his off watch, watching though he knew he should sleep, watching through lids that felt like heavy sandpaper, Luke finally said the magic words.

"They're not bluffing."

"Why the sudden decision?"

"It's no good, Lloyd. Bluff or no bluff, the fleet would have taken off as soon as they found the amplifier. The longer they wait, the closer we get to their velocity, and the more accurate our arrows get. They've been down too long. The ET has them."

"I thought so all along. But why hasn't *he* taken off?"

"In what? There's nothing on Pluto but singleships. He can't fly. He's waiting for *us*."

The conference was a vast relief to all. It also produced results. One result was that Woody Atwood spent a full thirty hours standing up in the airlock of the *Iwo Jima*.

Four million miles respectful had been good enough for the Belter fleet. It would have to do for Garner. His ship and one other came to an easy one-gee stop in midspace. The third had taken a divergent path, and was now several hundred miles above the still-shrouded surface.

"It's funny," said Smoky. "Every time you decide one of our ships is expendable, it turns out to be a Belt ship."

"Which ship would you have used, Old Smoky?"

"Don't confuse me with logic."

"Listen," said Masney.

Faintly but clearly, the radio gave forth a rising and falling scream like an air raid siren.

"It's the Lazy Eight's distress signal," said Anderson.

Number Six was now a robot. The *Heinlein*'s drive controls now operated the singleship's drive, and Anderson pushed attitude jet buttons and pulled on the fuel throttle as he watched the *Heinlein*'s screen—which now looked through Number Six's telescope. They had had to use the singleship, of course. A two-man Earth ship must be just what the ET desperately needed.

"Well, shall we take her down?"

Woody said, "Let's see if Lew's all right."

Anderson guided the singleship over to where the lead ship circled Pluto, turned off the drive and used attitude jets to get even closer. At last he and four others looked directly through the frosted, jagged fragments of Lew's control bubble. There were heat stains on the metal rim. Lew was there, a figure in a tall, narrow metal armor spacesuit; but he wasn't moving. He was dead or paralyzed.

"We can't do anything for him now," said Smoky.

"Right," said Luke. "No sense postponing the dreadful moment. Take 'er down."

The distress signal was coming out of a field of unbroken snow.

Anderson had never worked harder in his life. Muttering ceaselessly under his breath, he held the ship motionless a mile over the distress signal while snow boiled and gave him way. Mist formed on the *Heinlein*'s screen, then fog. He turned on an infrared spotlight, and it helped, but not much. Smoky winced at some of the things young Anderson was saying. Suddenly Anderson was silent, and all five craned forward to see better.

The *Golden Circle* came out of the ice.

Anderson brought the singleship down as gently as he knew how. At the moment of contact the whole ship rang like a brass bell. The picture in the screen trembled wildly.

In the ensuing silence, a biped form climbed painfully through the topside airlock in the *Golden Circle*. It climbed down and moved toward them across the snow.

The honeymooner was no longer a spaceship, but she made an adequate meeting hall and hospital. Especially hospital, for of the ten men who faced each other around the crap table, only two were in good health.

Larry Greenberg, carrying a thrintun spacesuit on each shoulder, had returned to find the *Golden Circle* nearly buried in ice. The glassy sheathing over the top of the ship was twenty feet thick. He had managed to burn his way through the hard way, with a welder in his suit kit, but his fingers and toes were frostbitten when he uncovered the airlock. For nearly three days he had waited for treatment. He was very little pleased to find Number Six empty, but he had gotten his message across by *showing* the watchers at her scope screen. All's safe; come down.

Smoky Petropoulos and Woody Atwood, doing all the work because they were still the only ones able, had moved the paralyzed Belters to the *Golden Circle* in the two-man ships. The four were still unable to use anything

185

but their eyes and, now, their voices. Lew's hands and wrists and feet and neck all had a roasted look where the skin showed through the blisters. His suit cooling system had been unable to cope with the heat during those seconds of immersion in flaming gases. If the gas hadn't been so extremely thin, some plastic connection in his air pack or his cooling system would surely have melted—as he would tell eager listeners again and again in the years to come. But that was for later. Later, the others would remember that they had all been wearing suits because they'd been forced to break their windshields, and that if Smoky and Woody hadn't found them that way they'd have starved in their ships. For now, they were safe.

Garner and Anderson were nearly over their induced paralysis, which now showed only in an embarrassing lack of coordination.

"So we all made it," said Luke, beaming around at the company. "I was afraid the Last War would start on Pluto."

"Me too," said Lew. His voice was barely slurred. "We were afraid you wouldn't take the hint when we couldn't answer your calls. You might have decided that was some stupid piece of indirection." He blinked and tightened his lips, dismissing the memory. "So what'll we do with the spare suit?"

Now he had everybody's attention. This was a meeting hall, and the suit was the main order of business.

"We can't let Earth have it," said Smoky. "They could open it. We don't have their time stopper." Without looking at Luke, he added, "Some inventions do have to be suppressed."

"You could get it with a little research," said Garner. "So—"

"Dump it on Jupiter," Masney advised. "Strap it to the *Heinlein*'s hull and let Woody and me fly it. If we both come back alive you know it got dumped on schedule. Right?"

"Right," said Lew. Garner nodded. Others in the lounge tasted the idea and found it good, despite the loss of knowledge which must be buried with the suit. Larry Greenberg, who had other objections, kept them to himself.

"All agreed?" Lew swept his eyes around the main lounge. "Okay. Now, which one is the amplifier?"

There was a full two seconds of dismayed silence.

Greenberg pointed. "The wrinkled one with both hands empty."

Once it had been pointed out, the difference was obvious. The second suit had wrinkles and bumps and bulges; the limbs were twisted; it had no more personality than a sack. But the suit that was Kzanol—

It lay in one corner of the lounge, knees bent, disintegrator half raised. Even in the curious shape of arms and legs, and in the expressionless mirror of its face, one could read the surprise and consternation which must have been the thrint's last emotions. There must have been fury too, frustrated fury that had been mounting since Kzanol first saw the fused, discolored spot which was the rescue switch on his second suit.

Garner tossed off his champagne, part of the stock from the honeymooner's food stores. "So it's settled. The Sea Statue goes back to the UN Comparative Cultures Exhibit. The treasure suit goes to Jupiter. I submit the Sun might be safer, but what the hell. Greenberg, where do you go?"

"Home. And then Jinx, I think." Larry Greenberg wore what Lucas Garner decided was a bittersweet smile, though even he never guessed what it meant. "They'll never keep Judy and me away now. I'm the only man in the universe who can read bandersnatchi handwriting."

Masney shook his head and started to laugh. He had a rumbling, helpless kind of laugh, as infectious as mumps. "Better not read their minds, Greenberg. You'll end up as a whole space menagerie if you aren't careful."

Others took up the laughter, and Larry smiled with them, though only he knew how true were Masney's words.

Or had Garner guessed? The old man was looking at him very strangely. If Garner guessed that, two billion years ago, Kzanol had taken a racarliw slave as a pet and souvenir—

Nonsense.

So only Larry would ever know. If the suit were opened it could start a war. With controlled hydrogen fusion as common today as electrical generators had been a century and a half back, any war might be the very last. So the suit had to go to Jupiter; and the doomed racarliw slave had to go with it, buried in dead, silent stasis for eternity.

Could Larry Greenberg have sacrificed an innocent sentient, even for such a purpose? To Larry plus dolphin plus thrint, it wasn't even difficult.

Just a slave, whispered Kzanol. Small, stupid, ugly: worth half a commercial at best.

Can't defend himself, thought Charley. *He* has no rights.

Larry made a mental note never to tell Judy, even by accident, and then went on to more pleasant thoughts.

What was he thinking? Garner wondered. He's dropped it now; I might as well stop watching him.

But I'd give my soul if I could read minds for an hour, if I could pick the hour.

MORE S-F
from
🅑🅑
BALLANTINE BOOKS